Mazeltov

Mazeltov

A NOVEL

Eli Zuzovsky

HENRY HOLT AND COMPANY

NEW YORK

Henry Holt and Company
Publishers since 1866
120 Broadway
New York, New York 10271
www.henryholt.com

Henry Holt® and ⓗ® are registered trademarks of Macmillan Publishing
Group, LLC.

Library of Congress Cataloging-in-Publication Data

Names: Zuzovsky, Eli, author.
Title: Mazeltov : a novel / Eli Zuzovsky.
Description: First edition. | New York : Henry Holt and Company, 2025.
Identifiers: LCCN 2024012043 | ISBN 9781250345271 (hardcover) |
ISBN 9781250345264 (ebook)
Subjects: LCGFT: Bildungsromans. | Queer fiction. | Novels.
Classification: LCC PR6126.U96 M39 2025
LC record available at https://lccn.loc.gov/2024012043

Our books may be purchased in bulk for promotional, educational,
or business use. Please contact your local bookseller or the Macmillan
Corporate and Premium Sales Department at (800) 221-7945, extension
5442, or by e-mail at MacmillanSpecialMarkets@macmillan.com.

First Edition 2025

Designed by Meryl Sussman Levavi

Printed in the United States of America

1   3   5   7   9   10   8   6   4   2

For my parents

God pities the kindergarten children,
The schoolchildren he pities less.
And the grown-ups he pities not at all.

—Yehuda Amichai

Contents

Mazeltov

I

SEPARATION

Eleanor

I t started with a tug on Adam's shoulder. Then another. And another one. When he finally gave in and crawled out of the dampness of his sleeping bag, the first thing he noticed was a yellow Tweety shirt, glowing in the dark. Then, above it, floating on the surface of a white, semi-familiar face, a pair of bushy eyebrows.

"Are you up?" she asked him.

"Now I am."

"Awesome," she whispered, handing him his glasses. "Let's get out."

She took him for a walk to find the moon. No one at the camp could say when exactly it had vanished. The only thing the Aleph troop scouts knew was that by two a.m. they couldn't see the yellow crescent gleaming in the sky above the forest. And Adam didn't have a choice. For Eleanor Fogel, whose wild idiosyncrasies were notorious among the campers, a moonless night was all too sad.

She was the biggest girl in Adam's class—not the oldest, but the tallest and the most developed. Like him, she was an only child. She spent most of her days alone. Her father had achieved a modest fame playing his electric organ at nursing homes across the country. Her mother worked as a couples therapist who saw her patients in the family's dark living room in Ramat Gan.

Every boy in sixth grade said that Eleanor was just as ugly as it gets. One of their classmates wondered whether she might be a sex doll with a soul. Their imaginations were ignited by the widespread rumor that she had given a blow job to Rani Ackerman, a tantalizing eighth grader, last Hanukkah on the music building's rooftop. He neither denied nor confirmed it; she was never asked. Soon enough, Eleanor became the subject of an unofficial contest among the boys, each attempting to outsmart the others with ingenious alternatives to her name. The list, which grew longer by the day, included gems like *Smelly-nor* and *Belly-nor* and *Elean-whore* and *Elea-norgasm* and *Eleanorgy*—the last one Adam's brainchild.

In Adam's eyes, she was astonishing, like an actress in an old French film. There was an otherworldliness to her that he admired. The life Eleanor led was tailored perfectly to her dimensions: large, breathtaking, unhinged, an unfailing wellspring of action and drama.

Her catchphrase, *Something happened*, was usually preceded by an enigmatic sigh. From time to time, she would storm into their classroom, disheveled, panting, forty minutes late, and go on to recite one of her fables. Every tale was thrilling—or, as his Mémé put it when he told her, *superbement étrange*. Most consisted of an inventive mishmash of some Argentinean telenovela Eleanor had glimpsed and the dry facts of her life. The stories featured a rotating cast of villains: cruel parents, shameless bus drivers and bikers, sloppy dentists and physicians, vicious rapists who had busted out of jail, and a vengeful clowder of red-eyed cats. The teachers, painfully familiar with the Fogel Tales, would half listen, nodding with impatience. They would order the bard to catch her breath and take her seat far in the back. Eleanor would smile and sigh, victorious, and readily obey. The students were engrossed. Later, they would go on to translate her adventures into doodles, secret notes, and bathroom gossip, savoring every delicious detail like forbidden candy and stifling a laugh.

But Eleanor's true talent was undoubtedly her voice. When she spoke, only the sharp-eared could identify the distinctive timbre of her words. Outside her classroom spectacles, she wasn't very talkative and refrained from saying anything unless she had no choice. But when she sang, she promptly ceased to be a joke. It was like magic, a sudden spotlight that reveals the beauty of a darkened stage. Eleanor transformed into a superhuman being, untouchable and sacred. Like a siren of some kind.

Every year, the drama students gathered in the schoolyard to perform the traditional remembrance service on Memorial Day with a zeal that seemed improper. It was on that makeshift stage where Eleanor launched her career. Standing at the front of a regimented line of flags and classmates, putting on the seriousness of an adult, she was the undeniable belle of the ball. Her greatest hits were ballads about dead officers turned angels and flowers on deserted graves that everyone could hum along to. Her voice, soft but unwavering, drove them all to tears—students, teachers, and parents alike.

Now she was leading Adam through a section of the forest that he hadn't seen before. The night was thick. He followed her, obedient, spellbound.

"Where are we going?" he asked.

"We need to find the moon," she told him.

"You said so, yes. But why?"

"The moon is gone, you know. And I can't sleep. So we are going, you and I, to bring it back."

This was their first real conversation in more than six years of acquaintance. They'd seen each other here and there, in the crowded corridors of school and on the sweaty dance floor of the occasional bat mitzvah. After all, their desks were just three rows apart in class. But there had been no prolonged communication between Adam and Eleanor.

"So what's your sign?" she asked him, bushwhacking through a stubborn bramble.

"I'm a Capricorn," he said as she was holding up a branch for him to pass beneath it. She was embarrassingly taller. "How about you?"

"I'm a Sagittarius," she said.

"What does it mean, to be a Sagittarius?" he asked.

"It's lots of things. Well, basically, I'm a gigantic personality.

I squeeze the juice out of life." She turned to look at him, the first time since they'd left the camp, and gazed a while, as if trying to measure his dimensions. "Wow, a Capricorn. That's rough."

"What? Why?"

"I mean, on most days, it's okay," Eleanor said. "Not the best, but definitely not a freaking Virgo or anything like that. But when there's no moon, that's when things get *really* tough for you. Without a moon, you guys are, like, literally fucked." She smiled and, after a silent moment, added, "My mother is a Capricorn. She's insane."

"My mother, too," he said. "Insane, not Capricorn. I think that maybe all mothers are. Some of them are good at making you forget it."

"My mother is depressed, I think," Eleanor said. "I mean, I know. She told me. And it's pretty hard to miss. She hates me. She kind of hates her life."

"I'm sorry, Eleanor."

She smiled; it was the first time he'd pronounced her name. He tried to taste it. His breath still had the tartness of his unbrushed teeth—he'd accidentally left his toothbrush by the bathroom sink back home—but still, her name was sweet inside his mouth.

When the silence of the woods began to feel too long, he asked, "Where did you say we're going?"

"I didn't," she responded.

"So?"

"I want to see the river."

"That's, like, a twenty-minute walk."

"And? Are you in a rush?"

He wasn't, so they walked. The air was wet. When Adam realized he could hardly see the bright lights of the camp behind them, he was relieved. Being an Aleph scout was never quite his thing. Not that he didn't try. His mother said that like anything on earth—people, places, the weird lasagna at that Greek place—it was worth at least one shot. "Give everyone and everything a chance," she told him. "At least until they disappoint you. And if they do, forgive them to the best of your ability, but don't forget."

He felt surprisingly at ease with Eleanor. There was something comforting about her way of moving through the world: her heavy footsteps; her deep, long breaths. With her, his restlessness somehow relaxed.

"Do you think it's better to be short and happy or tall and angry?" she asked him suddenly.

"I don't know," he said, and thought about it for a moment. "Maybe it's best to just be medium-sized and indifferent?"

She laughed. "Nah. I'd much rather be short and happy."

"Well, as a short, happy person, I'd love a chance to be tall and angry," Adam said. "You know. Just to see what it's like."

"Oh. Are you? Happy?"

"Yeah," he said, as if that were a given. "Of course. Are you not?"

Eleanor puffed her cheeks and made a farting sound. "I think that height is overhyped," she said. "Like, when someone says, 'I want my husband to be tall.' I just don't get that." After another empty moment, she added, "Sometimes I wish I were a mantis, or a bee."

Adam wasn't sure how to respond, so he shrugged, mumbling a pensive "huh."

Just before they reached the riverbank, Eleanor stood still.

"Can you see the moon?" he asked her, curious and baffled.

"I don't think so." She sat down on the ground and looked ahead, taking in the gushing of the stream. She sighed. "Too bad."

"I don't understand," he said. "Didn't you want to find the moon?"

"I think I'm over it."

"We can keep walking if you'd like. I'm happy to go—"

"Just sit down."

Adam looked into her eyes, attempting to decipher her expression. Now, up close, he could tell: she was just as lost as he was. For a moment, he saw a streak of anguish cutting through her face, brief but unmistakable, like lightning. He cleared his throat and sat down next to her, on a little patch of grass.

Eleanor froze. "So do you want?" she asked him.

"Do I want what?"

"To touch them."

"What do you mean?"

"My tits."

He swallowed. "Sure."

"Then why aren't you asking with your eyes?"

He looked away from her, pulling up a soggy piece of grass and crushing it between his fingers.

"I can touch yours, too," she said. Her voice was warmer.

"Mine?"

"Your dick. I mean, if you want me to."

Adam smiled. "I think I'm fine."

"What?"

"You don't need to touch it," he said, then quickly added, "Thanks."

"Thanks?" she said. "For what?"

"For offering, I guess. It's very nice of you."

"Why do you not—"

"Well, you can touch it, if you want. It's just . . ." He tried to find the right words in the darkness that surrounded them. "My mother made me swear that I would never be a schmuck, like, a gazillion times."

Eleanor chuckled, her white, slightly crooked teeth reflecting the blue brightness of the water. "What does that even mean, being a schmuck?"

"Like, you know. I don't know. Someone that makes girls do stuff."

"Sweet," she said. "I think you're sweet."

"Thanks," he said. "You too."

"Will you stop thanking me? I'm not doing you a favor."

"Oh, sure." He giggled. "Yes, of course. I guess you're right."

When the silence threatened to return, she cleared her throat. "So, do you wanna?"

"I don't think so."

"You said sure."

"I think I've changed my mind."

It seemed as if she tried to hold her breath. As if, by letting out the air, she would deflate. Then, to his great relief, she finally exhaled. "Is that because I am the most disgusting thing that you have ever seen?" she asked. "The kind of girl that makes you want to throw up in your mouth?"

Adam didn't know if he should look at Eleanor. The river hissed, making it extremely hard for him to think. "What? Are you kidding? Not at all." He tried to wrap her in his words, but knew they wouldn't reach her. Their eyes suddenly met. "I think you're very cool," he said. "Much cooler than the other girls, with their shorts and leggings and their sports bras. To me, you're much more beautiful."

She looked down at the ground, then turned to swallow him with an impatient kiss. His jaw gradually melted, its bones taking on the texture of a jellyfish. Her lips tasted of vanilla; they were soft and warm and bigger than he'd thought and slightly chapped. She grabbed his hand, slid it up her glowing shirt, and laid it on her bra, which was made of the finest lace Adam had ever felt. He liked its nubbiness. Slowly, like a thief, she disengaged her lips from his and let her hand glide down the stripes of his pajamas.

For a moment, nothing happened. They were sitting on the bank together, frozen, like they were waiting for a signal from someone. Then Eleanor started drawing soft, large circles on her right breast with his trembling hand. Adam helplessly recalled a recipe for challah bread he'd found in a yellowing notebook on his mother's kitchen shelf. It had his grandmother's name on it, the one who died years before his parents met. *Knead, pushing down and outward.* He shut his eyes so he could see the page more clearly. *Proceed until the dough is smooth and supple. Let it rise.*

After a while—he couldn't tell how long—the strange dance of their hands began to mock him, sending thin currents of failure up his fingers. His glasses had been fogging up. He didn't know what was to come and wasn't sure he wanted to. Eleanor began to squeeze his crotch. It almost hurt. His mind became an empty jar.

At first, he thought that she was moaning, putting on a show of pleasure, like the videos he'd seen on the screens of older boys in his computer class. But when he looked at Eleanor again, something had changed. A faint glimmer of tears was dripping down her chin. Her cheeks were burning red; her face was white.

He tried to focus on the stream, but couldn't. Like a dying engine, their movements started to slow down, then altogether ceased. She wiped her nose on his pajama sleeve and lay down on the earth. Her wide chest rose and fell. Her eyes were blank.

"Sorry," she said, curled up, staring at a mud puddle at her feet. "I saw you yesterday, alone, at dinner. You looked so silly, nibbling at your macaroni, eating it one by one. You stared at it as if it was the most precious thing you'd ever seen." She swallowed. "Boys would never kiss me. All they want is just the other stuff, which I don't like as much. Something made me think you might."

He lay down next to Eleanor, pressing a hand against her cheek, and gently kissed the stiff bone of her shoulder. It was cold. She didn't move. When her breath developed a consistent rhythm, he pulled his body away from hers in silence and rolled on his side. Adam took his glasses off and placed them on the ground, next to her ear. He tried to find the best position for his head, careful not to bother her. His temples throbbed. *Thump, thump. Thump.* His face was moist against the mud.

At last, he let his eyes drift shut. The night was getting softer, but still, the trees surrounding them were wet and dark. The air carried an unfamiliar scent of cow dung and eucalyptus. Adam wasn't sure if he was dreaming, but somehow, even through his eyelids, he could see the sun.

His Only Son

They wake up early, long before the sun comes up. His father stuffs a small black backpack in haste, making sure not to forget the water and the sunscreen. They drive for almost two hours, northbound, wordlessly.

Adam is sitting in the front, although he knows that's not allowed. But in his father's car, the world is vast—a wilderness—and rules often become recommendations. He can't remember whether it's a Mazda or a Ford. Perhaps a Volkswagen. He isn't sure and doesn't care enough to ask. His father is obsessed with cars and driving. Adam has been trying to memorize the different brands and logos. He's loved the challenge of remembering the funny names—Bugatti, Honda, Maserati—but he hasn't really been successful. One day, maybe.

Adam just turned six last week, but he has never felt so small. He leans his head against the car's cold window, then rolls it down, letting the wind blow through his long brown hair. He loves his hair. His father rests one hand on the steering wheel and holds a beer bottle in the other. The radio blasts a song that Adam hasn't heard before. It seems to be in conflict with the clock, whose red digits indicate 03:22. His father bobs his head and taps his fingers to the beat.

They pass dim gas stations and dormant towns whose names Adam can't recognize. The roads are desolate; he's never seen the country so devoid of life. Every now and then, their hands touch without meaning to, when they reach over the parking brake to grab potato chips.

The sky is hazy, and Adam left his new, round glasses on his nightstand, so he can't make sense of what he sees outside. He cups his hands and breathes against the window, writing his name and drawing small hearts in the steam. Peering through the letters, he thinks he sees a sheep, but then it's gone. He loses track of time, falling asleep and waking up over and over, until he can't quite draw a line between the long drive and his dreams.

"Where are we going?" Adam yawns.

His father turns to him, his only son, and smiles. "Do you know how much I love you?" his father asks.

"Me too," Adam responds, and falls asleep again.

When he wakes, the car is sitting in an empty parking lot. The world has grown a little brighter. He realizes that he is alone inside the car. Outside, his father pees and whistles, shaded by a tall green sign announcing, *MOUNT MERON—WELCOME!* He finishes, zips up his pants, and lights a cigarette, leaning on the trunk, which makes the whole car rock.

Adam remembers how, two mornings earlier, he overheard his parents argue in the kitchen. His father said he hadn't smoked in ages. His mother laughed and used a word that Adam found hilarious: *bullshit*. Now, still in the car, Adam stretches his arms and legs in all directions and tries to reach the ceiling. He gets out of the car and walks around the lot, singing a song under his breath so his father doesn't hear.

"Good morning, little man," his father says.

"Good morning."

"Don't stray."

"I won't." Adam continues singing.

The parking lot turns out to be more boring than he thought. Even the sky is dull today, not a single airplane to be seen. When Adam was a baby, he was obsessed with concrete mixers, seeking them everywhere he went. Or so his mother says. His father told him once that she can lie sometimes, like everyone he knows. But Adam is a big boy now. He hasn't given concrete mixers any thought in years.

"We'll start climbing soon," his father says. "I want to get there early."

Adam freezes. "Climbing? Where?"

His father grins. "You can hardly see it now," he says, "but we are at the bottom of what used to be, until the Six-Day War, the highest mountain in the country."

"And we are climbing it?" Even the thought of mountains feels exhausting.

"It is a very special place," his father says, "especially for *datiim.*"

"But we are not."

"Not what?"

"Religious."

"Right."

His father flicks his cigarette and stomps it out. Something in the sky has changed, and orange stains start peeking through the blue. His father grabs the backpack from the front seat of the car. "Come on." He clicks his tongue. "Let's go, little man." Adam pretends he hasn't heard. "Come on," his father says again as Adam walks around, drawing dust squares with his feet.

"Are you deaf or what?" His father grips his shoulder blade. "I said let's go."

Adam shakes his head from side to side, his refusal wordless, firm.

"You know what? Here," his father says, fumbling in his pocket. He takes out a silver lighter and offers it to Adam. "You can play with it as we climb. Just be careful." His father sighs. "God. Sometimes I forget you're only six."

They walk in silence. His father leads. Adam holds the lighter tight, flicking it on and off. He stops to marvel at the color of its flame, a wonderful blue-yellow-purple. He wants to touch it, but resists the urge. He doesn't feel like walking. When he loses sight of his father, he cries out "Dad?" and is answered by a reassuring "Here."

The trail stretches in front of them, brown and damp, its

end nowhere in sight. The air is sweet and cleaner on the mountain—it is a bright, crisp winter day—but Adam starts to miss the city.

"My feet hurt," Adam says, mimicking a robot. "I want to sleep."

His father doesn't laugh. "Quit it," he says.

"Why did I have to miss school today?" Adam asks. "We were gonna bake some kind of bread in science class. I don't understand. Why did I have to miss it?"

"Life can be a mystery sometimes," his father says. "Some things you just don't understand."

"Like what?"

"Like love."

"What does love even have to do with this stupid trip?"

His father stops and turns to him. He pulls out a plastic bottle from his bag with the label scraped off and hands it to Adam, ordering, "Drink this."

Adam reluctantly accepts the bottle. "It's warm. It tastes like piss," he says, using the back of his forearm to wipe the water off his chin.

"Who cares?" his father says. "Now drink it all. Come on, little man. Another sip."

When Adam finishes the water, his father puts the bottle back in his black bag and they resume their hike. Somehow, the leaves have gotten bigger and the trees have changed their colors; still mostly brown, now they are also red and green.

"Do I see cherries there?" Adam asks, enchanted, and stops to gape at a small tree that explodes in white. He tries to remember whether cherries grow up north. He knows that there are two main kinds in Israel: one sweet, one sour. Cherries are among the only fruits he likes.

"Could be," his father says. "Let's go. It's sunrise soon."

The earth beneath them smells of orchids. Above their heads, the sunbirds chirp.

"This is part of the National Trail," his father says after a while. "The last time I came here was ten years ago, maybe even more. Right before I met your mother. After my military service."

"Who did you come here with?" Adam asks.

"Alone. I walked for weeks, from the mountains to the desert, from Lebanon to Egypt."

"I thought you hated Lebanon. You said it was like hell."

His father laughs. "You know," he says, "sometimes I miss it."

"That's crazy," Adam says. "Did you ever get sad, walking alone like that?"

His father shakes his head. "The best two months of my entire life." He smiles. "Walking is good, especially when you are lost and not sure what to do. It helps you think. It heals you."

After a while, his father halts. Adam raises his eyes from the damp trail. They've reached a cliff. His father looks down the precipice and smiles. He mumbles, "This is it."

The day breaks into a whole new brightness. The air is clear, but the enormous fields and the highway at the mountain's foot are still covered in mist. His father puts his backpack on a rock. He digs through the bag and fishes out some of its contents: black sunglasses, a pack of broken crackers, toothpicks, a wallet. "Sit down," he orders, pointing to a tree trunk. Adam obeys him.

A glint inside the bag catches Adam's eye. He asks, "What's that?"

"It's a surprise," his father says. "Now close your eyes, okay?"

"Dad," Adam says, his eyes still open. "Does Mom know that we're here?"

"She's home. You'll see her later, when we're back."

"I wanna call her."

"We'll call her on the way home, little man. Now close your eyes for me."

Adam hesitates, then slowly shuts his eyes as firmly as he can, squeezing his eyebrows hard. He hears the mountain sigh under his feet. He hears some other sounds as well: the crunch of leaves, his father's breath, and then a snip, mysterious, next to his ears.

"Don't move," his father says and whispers words that Adam doesn't understand. Adam rubs his thumb against the lighter, careful not to break the spark wheel.

Something gently strokes his cheek, like a fallen leaf. Adam remembers there were no trees where they stopped. He tries to choke his curiosity but can't. He blinks open his eyes and instantly looks down. On the ground, he notices a tuft of hair. It's dense and brown. It's his. Adam looks up and sees two shining blades.

He yelps. "What are you doing, Dad?"

Holding a pair of scissors, absorbed by Adam's bangs, his father doesn't answer.

"Dad, stop," Adam says. "Please, stop. Why are you doing this?"

"I'm giving you a haircut, little man."

"But you're not even a barber," Adam says. "And I like my hair the way it is."

He tries to move, but his father puts a heavy hand on his right shoulder, muttering, "Stay still." Nimbly, with the ease of a magician, Adam's father cuts his long brown hair, sliding the scissors back and forth. Tufts fall around them, each like a muddy raindrop. Adam doesn't move. His cheeks begin to itch beneath his tears.

"I don't want a haircut, Dad," he says. "I just don't want it."

"It'll look great," his father says. "You'll see."

Adam slowly shakes his head. He grits his teeth. His father holds Adam's chin until it doesn't move. The cutting stops. The world is still. Adam exhales. His father fetches something from the bag. Adam hears a buzz like a malicious bee. His father is clutching an electric shaver. He holds it against Adam's head, moving it steadily. More thick locks fall to the ground. Adam follows them with his gaze, lamenting each and every one. The earth is littered with his hair, which has transformed into dark little hills.

"Why are you doing this?" Adam whispers. "Why are you doing this to me?"

"It's time," his father says, driving the machine down

Adam's nape. "Everybody thought you were a girl. Now you are handsome. *Clean.*"

The drone of the machine dies slowly. Adam tries to breathe.

"Usually, fathers come here with their sons when they turn three years old," his father says, covering Adam's new baldness with his hand. "A boy's first haircut. That's the tradition, is what I mean. They call it *halakeh*. A funny name. Then you can start entering the world of Torah."

"But I don't want to enter anything."

"My old man—your grandfather—never did it with me because he wasn't very interested in life. You didn't know him, he was a good man, but he hated what he called spirituality. He wasn't a terrific father, to be honest. I didn't do it when you were three years old because, well, you know. Because your mother wouldn't let me." His father pauses, stroking Adam's neck. "But now we're here, the two of us, father and son. Surrounded by God's creation and its beauty."

Adam tries to find the beauty that his father sees. He can't. The mountain is repulsive.

His father sits down on the ground and leans his head on Adam's shoulder. They watch the sun as it begins to make its entrance. In the vastness that sprawls beneath them, cars crawl along the highway, cows graze, farmers—tiny moving dots—walk through gigantic fields.

"We should take a picture for your mother," his father says and lets out a malignant laugh. "She'll be shocked."

Adam bends to the ground and holds the lighter against a tuft of hair, trying to ignite it. He watches the long strands curl, diminish, and slowly disappear.

His father leads him down a different path. It's barren and exposed. When they finally locate the car, Adam pushes the back of his seat down until it creaks. "Hey, easy there," his father says and then adjusts the rearview mirror. "Now, don't you want to see yourself?"

Adam pretends to be asleep.

They drive in silence. At traffic lights, his father puts a hand on Adam's knee and strokes it languidly. They park in front of a low-rise building with a sign that says in big red letters *SOLDIER DISCOUNT * BREAKFAST * ABRAHAM'S INN.*

The room is white, like in a hospital. It smells of floor cleaner and toast. They sit at the farthest table from the door, next to a small television set that plays a morning show. The hosts—a blond girl and a dark-haired guy in jackets—speak to a frowning man about the building of a giant fence. Adam turns his back to it. His father orders Turkish coffee.

"Do you know what you wanna get, honey?" the waitress, a tall, enthusiastic woman with an accent, asks Adam. He tries to guess her age and where she's from. She smiles at him.

"Isn't he the most handsome little boy you've seen in your entire life?" his father asks, removing sticky hairs from Adam's neck. "Now, isn't he?"

"He sure is," the waitress says and nods. "Would you like a pastry with that coffee?"

His father winks at her. "And one for this guy, too," he says. "The best pastry you have. And hot chocolate, please. With extra cream."

Adam doesn't speak. His father sips his coffee, shifting his gaze between his phone, his son, and the bright television set. "If you don't want it, I will drink it." His father gestures with his head toward Adam's mug. "I'm not your mother or your Mémé, you know. You can't play games with me."

It starts to rain. Adam straightens in his chair like a frightened lamb. The world grows darker in a heartbeat. He stands up and walks toward the window. The rain is pouring, turning everything outside into a blurry picture.

"Are you okay?" his father asks. Adam ignores him. He presses his nose against the window hard, until it hurts.

Then Adam dashes to the entrance, flings the door open, and runs outside, as if responding to a distant whistle only he can hear. His father follows him, alarmed. Adam lets the sweet rain fill his mouth. He waves his hands and thumps his chest with his small fists.

He has been waiting for this moment for too long—weeks, maybe even months. Ever since they learned that strange, new word in Bible class. *Yoreh.* The first rain of the year.

"Come inside," his father shouts, stooping under the narrow door frame of the inn. "Hey. Hey, Adam. Come on. Do you hear me?"

Adam roars and looks directly at his father, the first time since the mountain. His father smiles and, without warning, runs out and howls back at him. They are two jackals, wild, shivering and welcoming the rain together. People in the inn and in their wet cars gawk, but Adam doesn't care. His father laughs and lets the raindrops wash his face, his shirt, his jeans. He opens his arms wide, trying to create a shelter for his son. They hold each other tight, as if making an effort not to sink.

Merde

It was opening night, and all Adam could think about was that he painfully, desperately needed to take a shit. Too late now; he had already warmed up and been miked, hatted, powdered, heavily made up, and dressed against his will. The costume designer, thirty years in the profession by her own account, insisted that khaki overalls and wool felt berets had been the prevailing fashion among the vanguards of the fifties. Adam didn't dare challenge her, although he did wonder whether she was right (and knew almost for certain that she wasn't). He thought he looked ridiculous, a suspicion happily corroborated by his classmates, or fellow thespians, as their drama teacher, Vee, insisted that they call each other. They were thrilled to tell him that he looked like a stoned Middle Eastern Oliver Twist.

But then again, he had a solo. The first one of his life. A privilege that still seemed like a fiction. So obviously he had no right to say a thing.

Adam glanced at the pink plastic wall clock. The show would start in eighteen minutes. The dressing room was humming with activity. Too narrow for the number of sweaty bodies it contained, it had gray-yellow walls and six wide mirrors, which he consistently tried to avoid. Girls in tutus stretched and giggled, flitting around like goldfish in a pond. Techies dressed in black taped tiny wires to necks and cheeks and shoulders. Vee, making sure to bear-hug each and every one of the participants, blew kisses to the air. She kept scratching her hands, which were covered in layers of dead skin. Her strapless evening gown, blood red, was much more ceremonial than anything Adam had ever seen her wear. Coupled with purple lipstick, a velvet scarf, and brand-new glasses (same plastic frame, just in a different color: mauve), her look left little room for doubt: tonight was her party.

Adam admired Vee, despite the quirky ways that some found irritating but that, in his mind, made her unique. Everyone laughed at the fact that she had to supplement her income by teaching acting workshops in prison on the weekends. He thought it was so generous of her. He'd never seen a jail, although he always felt he should. When Vee was in the room, they all revered her like a goddess. There was that girl who even offered to massage her shoulders every now and then, which Vee refused. But in Vee's absence, she became an object of equal ridicule and pity. Everybody knew her real name was Vivian—their report cards gave away her secret at the end of every term—so why bother hiding it?

The country was about to turn sixty years old—Adam's

entire life times five. The school administration could find no better cause for celebration than the nation's anniversary. Originally, Vee had wanted to put on a gender-flipped production of *Fiddler on the Roof*, a long-held fantasy of hers. She'd always dreamed of playing Tevye. But the administrators talked her out of it. They said the musical was unsalvageably outdated and had a diasporic scent, which wasn't quite appropriate. (Adam had to check what "diasporic" meant online; he thought it was the name of a disease.)

Bummed yet never hopeless, Vee resolved to weave a new, exciting dream. She had it all planned out: a night of song and dance, deeply Israeli. A hodgepodge of patriotic gestures and nostalgia, just about digestible for the target demographic: Adam's classmates, eager to see their friends humiliate themselves onstage, and the parents, semi-liberal, Ashkenazi, and predominantly wealthy.

When he had seen his name on the cast list, which Vee had secretly taped to their lockers during gym class, Adam was flabbergasted. He was certain that the boys from 7B, his homeroom's rival class, were pranking him again. But the inaugural rehearsal, five days later in the Black Box, made it real. And if getting cast for the first time in his life was not enough (and he had tried a million times), the details only sweetened the discovery. He would portray the younger self of a character played by none other than Uri Shem Tov, a ninth grader, basketball player, and Greek god in the making.

Vee had a typically ambitious vision: a new rendition of a sixties song that would be a soul-stirring meditation on childhood under the austerity regime. Back in those early days of statehood, she explained, food, furniture, and clothing were meticulously rationed to tackle the crisis brought about by mass migration. That was the time, Vee told them, when her own beloved parents had left their unnamed native state and settled at a refugee absorption camp in Ofakim. "You kids can't even imagine what life was like back then," she said, refusing to reveal if she had already been born at that point. "You all are children of prosperity, which you naturally take for granted. But those folks were true heroes. Trailblazers. 'A land without a people for a people with no land' and all that jazz, right?"

After much deliberation, Vee picked "A Lone Streetlamp," one of the greatest hits of Hagashashim, the legendary comedy trio. Growing up, Adam spent most Saturday mornings staring at the television, eating his father's infamous Spanish omelet, and mouthing the dialogue of the trio's best-known skits. He did so avidly, consistently, with all his heart, although the humor was completely lost on him. But he knew Hagashashim were unanimously loved, especially by fathers, so he trained himself to like them, too. Who said that one must love only those few things that one fully understands? If Israel had a consensus (which Adam had already begun to doubt), Hagashashim were at the heart of it.

In Vee's plan, right before the song, Uri Shem Tov and two of his friends—who were just as thin and tall but lacked his majesty—would storm the stage. Three matchsticks, dressed in oversized fatigues, they would enact "The Drafted Car," one of the trio's most iconic scenes. In the sketch, an Israeli man—Uri, as usual, the lead—learns firsthand about military bureaucracy. He tries to reclaim his car, which the state has confiscated to support the war effort. (Or, as Vee described it, "Think of Ben-Gurion, Kafka, and Beckett having a three-some. In the army.")

After the sketch, the light would gradually change to signify a time warp. Cool blue neon would take over the yellow floodlights as Bach's Cello Suite no. 1 in G Major would blast through the speakers. The boys' expressions would promptly shift to neutral. They would walk backward in slow motion, mute, as seven ballerinas, dressed in blue and white, would whirl onto the stage and help them change into black suits and gray wigs. ("The ballerinas are the irresistible forces of Time, making fools of us all," Vee explained, misattributing the quote to Shakespeare.)

Then it would be Adam's time to shine, accompanied by Michael B and Michael G, both proud members of his homeroom's rival class, both professional child actors who'd signed with agents back when Adam was still learning the alphabet. Both were taller, skinnier, and blonder than he was. The former had risen to fame as the Boy Who Gets Slayed by What's Her Name in a recent production of *Medea* at the Cameri Theatre. The latter was known as the Sad Bald Kid from that cancer research ad that was popping up everywhere those days. That Michael loved to boast that he'd had to shave his crown of gold curls twice for the ad, being an *immersive* actor. It was with these two up-and-coming stars that Vee believed Adam belonged. She saw him there, under the blinding spotlight, center stage. *Medea*-Michael to the left, Cancer-Ad-Michael to the right, and Adam in between.

His solo was arguably one of the shortest in the history of Vee's productions. Merely seven words and he was done: "We heard the voices of our mothers," the *we* at an impossibly high pitch. It was sandwiched between two longer solos by the Michaels, each of whom enjoyed a full verse of his own. Then their adult selves—Uri Shem Tov and his friends—would emerge with the wisdom of old age, wearing their oversized suits and wigs. The ninth graders and the Michaels would share the remaining verses, while Adam would provide background vocals, humming a melody.

At last, he would become someone; he would be seen by everyone. He'd be a Theater Boy. One of the gang. Hooray! Adam was primed to dive into that warm pool of belonging. But as the days went by, he realized he couldn't swim.

"Sorry, folks, let's stop right there," Vee had said at one of their rehearsals, two weeks before opening night. She paused, filling the Black Box with suspense, and let her glasses theatrically slip off her nose. "Adam, honey, why do you tilt your head like that?"

"Do I?" Adam asked.

"Well, yes, of course," Vee said. "Haven't you noticed?"

The kids chuckled in unison. Two let out squeaky snorts, which startled him.

"I'm sorry," Adam winced, tilting his head back to the center.

"Apologies are of no use to us, my dear." Vee smiled. "Those we keep for Yom Kippur, right? But this is Independence Day, sweetheart. Rejoice. Have fun. And hold it still, now, will you? Thanks. Let's take it from 'the voices of.' Yes. When you're ready."

The rehearsal ended, as per usual, with a collective clap. No one was allowed to leave the room before they all managed to do it at the exact same time, which often took forever. After they did, Vee summoned Adam to her office. "Darling, a word," she said in passing, as his peers were tying shoes and murmuring. Adam followed Vee down the narrow hallway, imagining the words and tone she might decide to use when she uncast him. He hadn't even known she had an office.

More of a closet than a room, it looked exactly as he would have expected: lots of books on Sophocles and Brecht stacked everywhere—on her shelf, her chair, her wooden desk, and mostly on the floor—along with notes, newspapers, cigarettes, and a life-size Marlon Brando poster, black-and-white, highlighting the silhouette of his strong jawline and biceps. There was barely enough room for Adam to sit, so he remained standing at the entrance, leaning on her broken doorknob, smiling.

"Sweetie . . ." Vee sighed and lit a cigarette. "Are you okay? Is everything okay at home? You seem distracted, out of it, these days. Am I getting it right here?"

"I don't know." He shrugged. "I don't feel distracted, not really. I don't think."

"Do you have someone to talk to?" she asked. "A parent? Friend, perhaps? A therapist?"

"Yeah. Of course. My friends are awesome."

"Good." Vee seemed absorbed in thought. "I think I mentioned that Oscar Wilde quote at some point in class. Correct me if I'm wrong."

"Which one?" he asked. Quoting Oscar Wilde was a notorious Vee habit.

She remained silent for a moment, a faint smile tickling her lips. Then, suddenly, her eyes became two blazing suns. "Live!" She slammed the desk. "Live the wonderful life that is in you, darling! Let nothing be lost upon you. Be always searching for new sensations. Be afraid of nothing. Hear me? *Nothing.*"

"Oh, yes," Adam said. "I think you mentioned it when we did *A View from the Bridge* and you wanted us to—"

"I *believe* in you, Adam," Vee said, blowing smoke, still beaming. "I believe you are much better than you think. And I want you to go on that cursed stage and prove me right, prove everyone else wrong. And *live.* Will you do that for me?"

"I can try?"

"It's a deal. That solo that I gave you, it's brief, of course, like all good things in life. But it's no trifle, right?" She smiled, perhaps the widest smile he'd ever seen. "When you sing, the entire orchestra stops playing for a moment. We professionals call it *fermata* in our lingo. It looks like a cyclops eye when you see it on the sheet. You don't happen to read music, do you?" He shook his head, ashamed. "That's fine. And it is not too late to learn. I did it in my twenties. In any case, this fermata is *your* fermata, sweetie. Own it. I want them all to see you, hear you, feel you. The way I see you. The way I know that one day you will see yourself. Since I *believe* in you, Adam." She paused, putting out her cigarette and coughing. "And don't forget to memorize the hora choreography for Tuesday, fine? I'd hate to think that you might fall behind again." He nodded, dutiful. "Now, will you be a sweetheart and call Michael B into my office? I need to have a talk with that little donkey."

Adam obeyed, catching *Medea*-Michael just before he left the drama building. "Great job today, Michael," Adam heard Vee say as he tied his cleats outside her room. "Did we ever talk about that Oscar Wilde quote, darling?"

❦

Four deep metallic bangs thundered through the dressing room. Two ballerinas screamed. The show was just about to start. "Adam Weizmann!" called the stage manager, an upper-classman with fire-red curls and an elaborate headset. "There's someone here for you, banging on the door like some kind of lunatic. Stage Door Two. Hurry up, now, will you? Curtain will be up in seven," she said, her braces shining in the back-stage light. She whispered anxiously into her headset, "Sorry, yes, yes. Roger that. They're all amateurs here. It's out of my hands." She looked at Adam with a new layer of hostility. "Scratch that, Weizmann. Curtain's up in six."

Adam dashed to Stage Door Two, knowing what he'd find there. He unlocked the metal door, which let in a gust of summer wind. There she was: his best friend, Abbie, in a sleeveless floral dress, waving and smiling at him.

"Hey," she said.

"Hey," he said. "Why are you here?"

"You look cool. I like the hat."

"Thanks. Abbie, you should leave."

"I just wanted to say good luck."

"Are you insane?" Adam whispered, looking around to make sure the stage manager was out of sight and no one else had heard Abbie's words. "That's probably the worst thing you can say to a thespian before a show. That and, of course . . . *the Scottish*."

"Well, I am sorry I am not a thespian. And I actually have no clue who the Scottish even is. It's not my fault I was too fat for the dance department and too dramatic for the theater," Abbie said, pronouncing the last word with a thick fake British accent. "But you know what I always say. Those who don't want me are not worthy of me."

"You do say that a lot."

"Well, I believe it. And you should, too." She squeezed her lips, which, Adam knew, suggested that she was immersed in thought. "What should I wish you, then?" she asked.

"It's up to you. You can say, like, 'Break a leg.' Or as Mémé says, '*Merde*,' which is the French translation. It means, um, 'shit.'"

"Shit?" She laughed. Adam shrugged. "Well, *merde, mon cheri*."

"Thanks," he said. "Now leave. Please."

"Wait, Adam. Just a sec. I really have to hear about your dream."

"Abbie," Adam said under his breath as menacingly as he could. He knew Abbie's intentions weren't bad, but she was a ticking bomb of shame he needed to defuse. "Now is not a good time. Seriously."

"If not now, when?" she asked him.

"Well, later," he said. "After this."

The night before the show, for the first time in his life, Adam had been terrorized by dreams of boobs. They were everywhere he looked. In the fridge and in the cabinets, in his morning cereal bowl, little boobs in his shoes, in his locker, even in his nightstand's secret drawer. Boobs on his computer screen and in his Tamagotchi, boobs in his apartment building's elevator, boobs stacked in the back seat of his parents' Volkswagen. Most of them were independent of a body, but some—the most disturbing ones—were not. Several had their own teeth or noses. Some had mustaches and beards. One pair belonged to Vee.

Some of the boobs conversed. Many were grumpy, inexplicably. A few reminded him how dumb he looked in his pajamas. Others yelled swear words, called him names, and told him he was ugly. In one dream, he went to pee, and in an unfamiliar bathroom, he saw his mother, naked, lying in a gilded tub, smoking a cigar, and leafing through her favorite magazine.

"Would you like a puff?" she asked, smiling knowingly and rubbing the bubbles on her elbow, which was dripping soapy water.

"I don't think so," he said. "Thanks."

"Are you sure?"

"Yes. Pretty sure."

"That's a bummer, Weizmann. You're a bummer."

"Sorry."

Only when he woke up in a sweat did Adam understand what was so startling about the boobs—his mother's, and all the other pairs as well—beyond their sheer size and unexplained ability to speak. Like eyeless faces, they all lacked nipples.

That morning, Adam feverishly texted Abbie, as he often did. She was in biology class, learning about acid reflux. Like always, she kept her Nokia handy in her pencil case. Thrilled to see Adam's name appear on the small screen, Abbie responded within seconds. Theater Kids were typically exempt from lessons all through Hell Week—the five days prior to the show—a source of deep class antagonism. Even though Hell Week had turned out to be more pleasant than its name suggested, Adam could use some time alone with Abbie. He needed her advice and knew she'd be the best interpreter of dreams that he could find. They had agreed to meet at half past one at Schnitzeline, their favorite dining spot, for a quick debrief and French fries. They hadn't talked in days, so there was much to cover and unpack. But then, after a cataclysmic run-through, Vee announced that all participants were grounded until further notice, so Adam and Abbie couldn't meet.

"You'll give me all the details later," Abbie said now, leaning on the metal door. "But in the meantime, I just need to know one thing. Was I in your dream, or was I not?"

"What? Of course not," Adam said. "What do you mean?"

"What do you mean, 'what do you mean'? 'Of course not'? Why is that so obvious?"

"Can we talk about it later?"

"Sure. Just one last question. Who else was in it?"

"In my dream?"

"No, in the finale of *The Biggest Loser*." Abbie sighed. "Are you sure I wasn't in it?"

"What? No. Eeww."

"What? 'Eeww'?"

"I mean, just, no, I didn't dream about your boobs," he said. "But I really cannot talk right now, Abbie. Please. I need to concentrate. We have a show in, like, three minutes."

Abbie swallowed. "I bet those anorexic ballerinas were in your dream. Little bitches. Were they?"

"They were not."

"Liar."

"I'm serious."

"So you don't think I'm hot?" she asked. "Just say it."

"What? No. I mean," he mumbled. "Yes. Hell yes. You are. Absolutely."

"I am . . . What?"

"Hot. You're super hot."

"Thanks." She blushed. "You're hot, too. Even though you're literally the only boy I know who is afraid of tits."

"What? Abbie, I am not afraid of—"

Three organ sounds announced the imminent beginning of the show. Abbie pecked him on the cheek.

"Are you nervous?" she asked.

"Nope," Adam said.

"Why do you look so nervous, then?"

"I just really need to pee," he lied, not feeling in the mood to talk about his bowel movements.

"All righty," Abbie said. "It's time for me to leave. You'll be amazing, *mon petit ami*. Before you go onstage, just close your eyes and give yourself a hug, pretending that you're me, okay?"

He sighed and nodded. She waved goodbye and joined the herd of people rushing to the auditorium. Adam couldn't bear to look at them. He didn't want anyone else to see him in his costume; Vee had claimed that actors pre-performance were not unlike a bride before her wedding. He pushed the door with all his might, until it closed with a resounding *bam*. His stomach made a funny sound. He really had to take a shit.

Then he heard a snicker—almost indistinct, but full of spite. He turned around. Behind him, Adam found a ballerina, two years younger than himself but just about his height, folding her arms and smiling. She wore too much mascara and had red nail polish on her fingers. She didn't say a word. She didn't blink.

"Weizmann!"

Downstairs, the stage manager was livid, her braces gleaming in the darkness. "Are you serious? Why are you still up there? Come down immediately, okay? Gosh. Vee is already giving her speech." She glimpsed at her turquoise wristwatch, pressing the middle button that made it glow. "How can you be so unprofessional? You have a show in, like, two minutes."

Adam walked back to the dressing room, disgraced; the glances made it clear that everyone had heard the stage manager's rebuke. Vee was already deep into the emotional chapter of her pep talk, for which she was known throughout the theater community. Some said she used to be a promising young actress in the eighties, with concrete job offers from every self-respecting theater from Beersheba to Haifa. Her career was cut short by a speeding military truck that hit her just outside the National Theatre, which accounted for the deep scar on her neck and her slight limp. (She, of course, preferred to attribute both to her unflagging commitment to Method acting when she played Laura in *The Glass Menagerie*.) The magic of the theater, of which she'd spoken so extensively, was clearly in the air. Six kids—including one of the Michaels, who was holding on to the shoulder of the other—were tearing up and nodding.

"Okay, my darlings." Vee shifted gears. "The time has come. They need me up in the control booth, so I shall leave you to it. Bye now. You are fabulous creatures, each and every one. And I beg you: whatever happens on that stage tonight, please try to find your light, or else . . ." She relished the silent moment of anticipation, so rare among the youth, and flashed a smile. "Never mind. You will be grand, I know. You will. The Great Work Begins."

Her statement stirred something in Adam's bowels, which made a noise that sounded like a trumpet underwater. No one heard it, much to his relief. Except for one kid. While everybody gathered in the middle of the room, forming a perfect circle around Vee, clasping hands and yelling, "Break a leg!" the red-nailed ballerina grinned at Adam. She stood on the opposite side of the room, hands still folded, like the villains in the Westerns that his father loved. What did she want from him?

Before Adam even noticed, Vee had vanished and the dressing room had gone pitch dark. He wondered one last time whether he should sneak into the restroom just before the show began, but it was too late. An unknown hand tapped his shoulder. Time to go onstage; the gallows were waiting. When the accordion began to play, the lights went down, the curtain rose, and the first group number started, featuring the entire company.

The first act went quite smoothly—surprisingly so, given that Adam's stomach kept reminding him that it was seriously unhappy. The news behind the scenes was that Vee had zero notes for them, an occasion as rare as a meteor shower in the Negev desert. The thespians were thrilled. After the first number, Adam began to tiptoe toward the farthest bathroom he could think of. But an evil whisper stopped him.

"Where do you think you're going?"

The stage manager blocked his way, pointing with her head toward the opposite wing of the theater. Her reprimanding eyebrows made it clear that Adam had to stay. Beyond his duties as a full-time actor, he had been pressured into agreeing to double as a techie, helping with transitions and special cues. Back then, it seemed a sensible decision, a form of solidarity with his underprivileged classmates. Why did he always feel the foolish need to volunteer? He tried to negotiate and beg; he even offered to find someone to replace him—to no avail. "You wanted fame?" the stage manager asked, pressing her headset with her hand. "Well, fame costs. And right here is where you start paying . . . in sweat, my dear."

After fifty minutes—the longest in his life—the first act ended. The grand finale was his classmates' high-spirited rendition of the "We're All Jews" number from the film *Kazablan*, an old-time classic, from which he was exempt. Wearing rags and headscarves, they portrayed Jewish folk of various backgrounds at the marketplace, swinging their heads from side to side, throwing fake oranges and potatoes in the air, a Zionist Cirque du Soleil. "We're all Jews, every one. We all live under the sun," they sang together, joyfully.

It was intermission now. In the overlit foyer, parents and kids were gossiping, comparing unlawful pictures (photography was not allowed), helping grandparents find restrooms, and buying overpriced, underbaked goods to help fund the building of a new gym.

Adam was sitting in a backstage bathroom stall, his thighs giving in to the soothing coldness of the toilet seat. He wanted to sink into the filthy water and disappear forever. At least he hadn't pooped his pants. He still couldn't believe his luck. The shit gushed out of him, liquid and acrid. Adam let himself exhale. He was grateful to be left alone. But his solitude was promptly violated when the bathroom door slipped open and two boys waltzed in, chuckling.

"No way," one of them exclaimed. Adam recognized this voice: Cancer-Ad-Michael.

"And the craziest thing is that the faggot is so terrified of boobs that he didn't even dream about his friend's little titties," the other voice—*Medea*-Michael—said. Adam held his breath. He heard the boys open their zippers, the prelude to their urination duet. He shut his eyes and listened to their piss.

"Oh, right. Wait, what's her name again?" Cancer-Ad-Michael asked.

"I can't remember. She's the year above us," *Medea*-Michael said. "Big ass, crazy eyes like a maniac. You know? I heard she let Ackerman finger her behind a bush after that Purim party."

"Whoa," Cancer-Ad-Michael yelped. Adam could hear his smile. "That's sick."

"I would tap that," *Medea*-Michael said, and added, after giving it some thought, "Yeah, for sure, why not?"

"Big deal. You would literally tap anything. If you could, you'd even tap your mother, perv."

The streams of urine stopped. Adam heard their footsteps heading toward the exit. "Oh, sure, you mean *your* mother?" *Medea*-Michael asked, offended. "Because that's what I did last night. And I am telling you, she is hot as shit."

The voices dwindled to a low hum as the door closed

forcefully behind the Michaels. They didn't even wash their hands, which neither surprised nor bothered Adam. Something else was on his mind: the ballerina. Little bitch. The situation worsened when he went outside. Like at a crime scene, the kids were huddled around one of the wide mirrors. The room buzzed with the excitement only rumors could create. On the mirror, he saw a sentence written in red letters:

ADAM WEIZMANN IS AFRAID OF TITSSSSS

He slid back into the darkness of the bathroom. Pushing his ear against the door, Adam listened to the laughter, the *no way*s, and the *oh my god*s, a nauseating fizz. The organ thundered thrice, summoning them all to their respective places. He knew exactly where he had to be and what was next. What he feared was now upon him. First the sketch and then "A Lone Streetlamp." His *chant du cygne*.

He wet his face, his hands, his hair. He needed time. But there was none. Nor was there air. So he just sat down on the floor, waiting for the pageant of his humiliation to begin.

When the dressing room grew dark, Adam snuck upstairs and hid in the stage-right wing. The Michaels were already there, as he had expected, mouthing the dialogue between their older selves while waiting for their turn to finally perform. The audience was roaring, drunk with laughter. Uri Shem Tov and his friends were killing it. Adam remembered Abbie's tip about what he should do before he went onstage.

He wondered where her seat was in the theater; he couldn't see her through the fog, the thespians, and all the artificial light. He tried to give himself a hug, when suddenly he felt a strong tug on his sleeve.

"Come on, dude," *Medea*-Michael whispered, his blond head soaked in neon light. "We're up. We got this."

Adam let go of his body, allowing it to be dragged through the flock of flying ballerinas and placed onstage like a mannequin. He stood between the Michaels as rehearsed. The tone had clearly changed; the auditorium fell still. Even though he knew he shouldn't, Adam looked into the wings. To his left, he saw Uri Shem Tov slip into his suit, glowing with post-sketch pride, bare-chested and broad-shouldered, swimming in deep blue light. The sight was otherworldly. Adam blinked, and blinked again, but he could have sworn that Uri Shem Tov was grinning at him.

The ninth grader's face took on a strange expression. Something was happening behind his lips. Uri Shem Tov clenched his hand and raised it. He drove it from one side to the other, in slow motion, brushing it against his jaw, time and again. He moved it softly, pretending he was sucking on a big bulge in his mouth as he pressed his tongue against the inside of his cheek.

Then Adam saw it: mockery—no, worse, disgust. No. It was loathing.

The lights went up, revealing a young trio in khaki. A wistful tenderness rippled through the audience. There was a flash. And then another one, more distant, brighter. The orchestra began to play the melody that Adam knew too well. He heard a violin; it moved him. But he couldn't move his body. His mouth became a desert. Hot. The stage was hot. And dry. He was so thirsty. The makeup on his smooth face burned. He couldn't speak. His eyes were swelling with some liquid. He felt a huge, wet lump materialize inside his throat. He scratched his thigh and looked around, hoping he could smile. He couldn't do it.

Somehow, he registered it was his turn to sing, but still he couldn't move. The orchestra fell silent. *Fermata.* Adam's time to shine. An entire auditorium held its breath. His mother was probably there, hiding a camera and tearing up. His father, maybe. Probably not. And Abbie. And behind the blinding lights, shrouded in haze, Vee in the control booth, an angel watching over him. She'd wanted them to see Adam. What did they see?

It was his moment now. The Michaels turned to look at him.

He didn't sing. He didn't sigh or blink. He didn't know how long he stood there like that, frozen, wanting to die. The song came to an end. The lights went out. The audience may or may not have clapped. All he could see was the faint glimmer of the stage manager's watch in the darkness, which was thick and hot and full of malice.

II

THRESHOLD

What's Wrong with Abigail???

A long, long time ago
(**Just kidding—2009**)

In a galaxy far, far away
(**Also known as Israel**)
(**And/or Palestine,**
depending on your politics)

To the best friend I've ever had and ever will,

I truly can't believe this day has come. It feels like we've been waiting for it our entire lives. At least for as long as we've known each other—five years, three months, and twelve days, to be accurate. That's almost 40 percent of your entire lifetime, and about 36 percent of mine. Even though, as you know, we only officially became true friends three and a half years ago. Which was surely the best day of that year.

There are so many things I want to tell you, Mister Adam Weizmann, and sometimes I feel like the world moves faster than my thoughts and I barely even have time to catch my breath. So, even though it's far too early and I'm half asleep, this is why I'm writing you this letter—a token of my never-compromising friendship—which I hope you read at the end of what will definitely be the most amazing day.

As you know, I'm the biggest fan of lists. I think it was you who even said I was "an addict" (which I am NOT, I can stop at any point, I promise). So I thought it would be nice to start this letter with a little recap of our friendship. So that when we eventually get old, which hopefully will never happen, we can read it and have a laugh about our stupid selves.

WHAT MAKES ADAM AND ABIGAIL
TRUE BEST FRIENDS?

1. They both agree that Halloumi cheese is beyond all doubt the single most disgusting food ever to come into existence, period, end of debate. (And they have nothing against the Cyprians who traditionally eat it—they've never even been to Cyprus—so it's by no means racist.)
2. Both tried—and failed—to get into Renata's choir. They've totally moved on, of course. That was also how they met.
3. People often say about them that:
    a. *They are* . . .
        i. *smart way beyond their years.*
        ii. *like the friends from* Friends, *but cooler and less problematic.*
        iii. *like yin and yang.*

b. *Those who don't know them could think that they're siblings, but they're not even related!!!*

c. *Why don't they just get married?* (This one often comes from Shula, Abbie's crazy grandmother. She's a character.)

4. Both of them hate gym class, particularly dodgeball, which is undoubtedly the worst game in the universe.

5. Their favorite Beatles song is, obviously, "Hey Jude" (even though they HATE the Hebrew version, in which Jude turns into Ruth for some unknown reason). Their least favorite one is "Revolution 9," of course, which is basically just a bunch of weird sound effects and noises that pretentious farts like to call *experimental music.*

6. Both find Hitler more funny than scary—the mustache makes it hard to take him seriously—but they do their best because they know they should.

7. Both tend to bite their nails (though Abbie much more often).

8. Both like piercings but despise tattoos, love *Harry Potter and the Chamber of Secrets* but hate *Harry Potter and the Deathly Hallows*, and take showers only after five p.m.

9. Their favorite season is winter (except for February—way too damp), primarily by virtue of their birthdays (Adam in January, Abbie in March).

10. One day, maybe even as they read this letter, they'll both be based in Paris (because being "based" somewhere makes it sound as if they actually do something

that matters), in the same building but in separate apartments, ideally on the same floor, with doors facing each other and identical cute doorbells. And huge matching red windows overlooking a big old church named after some obscure Christian saint or a revolutionary who was executed just outside their building. And they'll be fluent in French (Adam will teach Abbie after he finally masters the language) and will practically live at the best museums in the world (she'll do her research and also be so rich she'll be able to cover ticket costs and transportation; Adam will never need to pay—well, maybe just for the baguettes, we'll see). And they'll both have French partners who'll be very different from each other but will also get along, truly, not in a fake French way. And they'll all go on vacations in the south of France, the four of them, like in the movies, and eat so much stinky cheese and grapes that they'll want to throw up (but they won't because it will also be delicious).

Remember that time when I was so sad and I stayed in my room, eating Lucky Charms and chocolate-coated almonds, and I wouldn't stop listening to that Avril Lavigne song on loop all day? I thought I gave myself diabetes with all the sugar, but then I looked it up and realized that wasn't how it worked. Remember how you saved me then? You'll probably say that I'm exaggerating, but I am absolutely not. I locked my door and wouldn't let anybody in, not even the pizza man, who was delivering the food that I myself had ordered.

But when you showed up at my house, I let you in because I knew you were the only person in my life who actually cared. And then you walked into my room and I was so afraid. I thought you'd realize that I had faked my coolness all along and would finally stop being my friend. I had a feeling that would happen one day. There was so much noise inside my head I couldn't hear my thoughts. I knew my room smelled like a stable (at that point, I hadn't taken a shower in three and a half days). But you didn't judge—you never do—not even for a moment. You smiled in your crooked, awkward way, tilting your head, and you told me I looked cute, even after eighty hours of isolation and self-hate.

Then you saw the chaos of my desk and asked me, *Oh, hey, what's that*, and I had totally forgotten that my lists were there, all of them, I think, scattered like dead bodies at the murder scene. That was way before I told you about my Problem. I was so afraid you'd hate me, which you never will, I know, but which I didn't know back then. You were confused, you must have thought I was a weirdo (which I am, admittedly), you said, *What's up with all the lists*, and I smiled and mumbled something stupid, but you insisted, as you always do, and asked, *What did you say*, and I responded, *Well, I guess I just like lists*, and you asked, *Lists, ha ha, what do you like about them*, and you were genuine, unlike most people in this world, you were silent for a while, actually waiting to hear what I would say. So I smiled again, but this time didn't say a word, and even though you were probably eleven and I was maybe twelve, you realized you'd accidentally touched an open wound and didn't want to shove your hand inside it, you're always so polite and sensitive and sweet and kind, and so soft-spoken, which probably won't get you very far in a slaughterhouse like Israel, but which is part of that mysterious thing that makes you the best best friend. And now, when both of us are old and wise, we've been through so much since that day, *mon petit ami*, I feel like I owe you an answer.

WHY DOES ABIGAIL LIKE LISTS?

1. Lists are the incarnation of order.
2. Lists make me feel like I know what I'm doing, or at least like I have some sense of control over all the noise and mess.
3. When done correctly, lists can be quite beautiful, especially if you `experiment` with *different* fonts.
4. I like numbers and geometry and math (I know you don't, which I still don't understand).
5. I'm always terrified of things being forgotten (birthdays, homework, promises). Lists can make forgetting pretty much impossible, or at least unlikely, which is nice.
6. Lists make me feel less anxious—especially if they're comprised of three, five, seven, ten, or thirteen items—which my therapist, Ayelet, says is part of my Problem.

7. I remember reading on a blog that some Italian guy said that lists make infinity comprehensible. I personally think that infinity is pretty cool and kind of key to understanding how the strange mechanisms of our world work, so it is something I would like to comprehend.

Then there was the time I came back home from school and my dad was having sex with a red-haired woman I didn't know on our kitchen counter. She clutched its corners with her long pink fingernails and shrieked. I thought I'd seen her once before but wasn't quite sure where and was too terrified to ask. I stopped eating for a week because every single item in our fridge smelled like her. Remember how I tried to run away, stuffing my Hello Kitty bag with chewing gum and chocolate? You saved me back then, too.

The crazy thing is—and I don't think I've ever told you this—that Liat knew about it all along, those things about my dad. I hate him. And I hate her, too, of course, but in a different way.

She's so dumb, really. It kills her that I've started calling her Liat. I think it's hilarious. She says it breaks her heart, that doing something like this to your own mother is alienating and cruel and deeply upsetting and that I should know that I'll regret it one day. Okay. Maybe she'd rather be called *bitch*? I wouldn't be surprised. She asks me why I do it. My question is, why would you get married to a guy when you know that he's a piece of shit? That he clearly hates your guts and will forever treat you like a servant? Literally. So stupid. And so damn blind. She's the only woman I've ever met who actually undoes—like, actively—the achievements of feminism every single day. Actively, and consciously. Now, *that's* upsetting.

The problem is that, from the moment men are born, they're told that they're the best. Women, on the other hand, are told that they're the worst, but they could overcome their fatal flaws if only they could make men give a damn. Or, in better cases, they learn that men are genuinely not that great, but that they can make men better if they only try. Yikes. That is exactly why girls like Eleanor act the way they do, and always will, until our silly civilization ends. Which I guess is not that far into the future. It's not even the women's fault. Just think about it. Even my name. *Abigail.* Which in ancient Hebrew means *my father's happiness.* Like, seriously? What about *my* happiness? Does anybody even care?

But Abigail was actually a pretty awesome lady. I mean, the Abigail I'm named after, the one from the Bible. In fact, she was so cool god gave her an entire speech. Which I guess in Bible time was a big deal for a woman. (Check it out! Samuel 25! It's INSANE.)

Abigail had both the beauty and the brains. Like most women, she married a douchebag, probably for lack of better options. But eventually, things worked out for her, because she ended up with King David (who was a douchebag, too, but of a different brand, and had a palace). Most importantly, Abigail prevented bloodshed—the best thing anyone can do. She convinced King David not to kill her first husband despite his uncontrollable male ego and everything his brainwashed, bloodthirsty advisers told him. How cool is that, *mon petit ami*?

SOME OTHER AWESOME JEWISH LADIES
(A PARTIAL LIST)

1. RBG. (Not to be confused with RPG, like the one your dad told us almost hit his tank in Lebanon in 1988.)
2. Golda Meir.
3. Anne Frank!
4. Grandma Shula, who at sixteen was a medic in the Independence War.
5. Queen Esther, or her modern incarnation, Britney Spears.*
6. Sarah Aaronsohn. (A spy! And in the 1910s! Who would rather shoot herself in a bathroom than rat on her friends! That's basically the definition of awesomeness, right?)
7. Princess Diana.*
8. Geulah Cohen (even though she's a Likudnik).
9. Natalie Portman.
10. My therapist, Ayelet. And Barbra Streisand, too, actually, when I think about it.

Remember that blue-eyed tour guide from the space museum who told us that at the end of the day, everyone was

---

*Not officially Jewish (I don't think?), but awesome nevertheless.

made of stardust? He made it all sound beautiful and simple, didn't he? You said he was amazing. And I agreed, of course. Who wouldn't? I've never told you this, but as we were leaving the planetarium, he grabbed my ass. I didn't do anything. You'd think I would. I thought so, too. I always told myself I would beat up anyone who tried to touch me, maybe even sterilize the guy once and for all, teach him a lesson he wouldn't forget. But I just stood there, frozen. I wondered if it might have been a dream. I know it wasn't.

I'm going on a tangent here. I'm sorry. It's your birthday! YAY!!!

Remember when we had dulce de leche ice cream with your Mémé by the broken fountain at the commercial center? Remember how you told me I was the happiest person you'd ever met? I didn't respond back then, you must've thought I was too focused on my ice cream, which I absolutely was, but the truth is that I'm incredibly unhappy. You'd be amazed.

SO, YOU'RE PROBABLY ASKING YOURSELF NOW, WHAT'S WRONG WITH ABIGAIL, THE HAPPIEST PERSON I'VE EVER MET IN MY ENTIRE LIFE???

(*Mon petit ami*, I think you're finally ready for the gory details, now that you're a man.)

1. Abigail is too tall and angry. And, of course, too fat.
2. Abigail likes one person (AW, a.k.a. you) and basically

hates all others, or at least most people, especially boys, especially her age.

3. Abigail desperately hopes that craziness is not hereditary, because her parents are insane, and it only gets worse as they grow older, so good luck with that.

4. Abigail is really good at math, like Math Olympiad level (not to brag), but bad to medium at basically everything else.

5. Abigail has far too many hairs on her legs and belly and arms and armpits.

6. Abigail would like to know how to become a better dancer and, more specifically, how to do splits.

7. Abigail would also like to be a better writer.

8. Abigail's feet are shockingly uneven (right bigger than left).

9. Abigail does NOT care about things that girls her age are expected to enjoy, like lip gloss and guys and modern dance (e.g., she is still yet to read *Little Women*—yes, yes, an all-time classic, sure, but why so many pages, sister?).

10. Abigail keeps losing things she really needs (most recently: calculator, phone, Grandma Shula's necklace).

11. Abigail would like to love pets, but unfortunately, she finds the vast majority of them gross. On a good day, she can get along with hamsters if they're well-behaved.

12. Abigail is addicted to Oreos and peanut butter (*They tried to make me go to rehab* . . .).

13. Abigail will be fourteen in two and a half months and

she still hasn't gotten her period. (Liat says that it's a side effect of medicating.)

Liat has constantly been telling me that I should have more friends, which only proves that she's a fool. She has more problems than I have beauty marks (which, as you know, are many). Her fatal flaw, which my therapist, Ayelet, has brilliantly identified, is that she lacks any sense of nuance. And she never thinks before she speaks, which REALLY drives me crazy. Like, not even a bit. If she had a middle name, it would probably be Cunt. Also, she is *extremely* old-fashioned, even though she desperately tries to make herself look modern.

PRELIMINARY EVIDENCE/SMOKING GUNS/ SOME UNBELIEVABLE EXAMPLES THAT WILL MAKE YOU GASP

1. IN THE CAR

ME: *Hey, can you play that song I like from the Amy Wine-house album?*

LIAT: *Honey, I really don't think you should listen to the music of that drug dealer.* (That's literally libel.)

2. AT THE ORTHODONTIST'S

DR. FLEITMAN: *We can easily fix that pretty smile, sweetheart, if that might be of interest.*

ME: *No thank you, doc!* Adios!

LIAT: *But wait a minute, honey. Why not? We can at least*

listen to what Dr. Fleitman has to say. Boys don't really like girls with crooked teeth—ha ha—or at least they didn't back in my day. (...)

3. IN THE PARKING LOT OUTSIDE THE GROCERY STORE

LIAT: *Don't you think that Black gentleman who helped us put our stuff in the bags smelled kind of strange?* (Her actual words.)

ME: *Liat are you serious with me or what that is like the most racist thing I have ever heard please stop this Nazi bullshit!!!!!*

So last week I decided that I don't want to have children. I probably most likely pretty surely won't ever get married either. Even though that's more negotiable, I guess. Depending on my future partner and the circumstances of our lives. I also decided that I would stop eating Nutella because that famished woman on TV who was an expert said it made you fat. And that I want to earn a ton of money in my life. Like, buckets. I still need to figure out the details, including how and where I'll put it. But if there's something that I've learned these past few months, it's that money is much more important than we like to think. Especially if you're a woman.

Like, take me, for example. The only thing that's keeping me from moving out is the fact that I literally have zero cash (except for almost three hundred shekels that I hide under my pillow, but that's not nearly enough these days). I mean, if you think about it, it's not impossible—after all, your mother did it when she was just about our age. But I guess that was kind of different, because it was the eighties and her own mother died and her father was a scumbag, yada yada yada. ~~Sometimes I wish Liat would die, too.~~ Also, she's your mother, i.e., the most one-of-a-kind, bigger-than-life person I know (mostly in a good way).

The last time I talked to her when I dropped by your place, she told me all about how difficult your dad had been (what's new?), which I COMPLETELY understand. He's such a wreck. She also gave me a box of those oatmeal cookies you pretend to like (which you can stop doing, by the way, she's onto you—I swear I didn't tell her anything!!). Then, just before you came back from scouts, she said I should consider being a therapist when I grow up. Everybody says that. *You're just so good with people.* Well, I'm also good with kids, does that mean I should be a mother??? I actually think I'd like to be a lawyer. Or a cop. Maybe a judge, like RPG. I mean, like RBG. Ha ha. I want to save the world, not to destroy it. LOL.

I've been *obsessing* over justice these days. I've also been obsessing over crunchy peanut butter with no sugar and no palm oil. And Manuel from *Verdad o reto*, which, as you know, your friend here has been watching like a druggie. He and Luciana Espósito make *such* a pretty couple. DID YOU KNOW THEY ARE TOGETHER IN REAL LIFE? I think she's pretty mediocre.

I'm always hungry for some reason. And I barely get any sleep. Usually less than five hours, which is, scientifically, not even close to being enough, and will most likely interfere with my puberty. I often lie in bed with my eyes wide open, stressing over every atrocity I can imagine. Do you sometimes catch yourself and realize the world is 99 percent made of danger?

A HANDFUL OF POTENTIAL DEATHS

1. I could perish in an Iranian nuclear bombing (or a plane hijack or arson, or just a normal act of terror, like an exploding bus or a missile attack or a stabbing at a mall or something like that).
2. I could die of my wounds after a terrible car accident for which no one will be prosecuted because our justice system sucks. Or I can stay alive, but become disabled, like my dad's cousin Sharon.
3. I could be kidnapped and locked away for years in a basement, where I'll surely be forgotten.
4. I could die or get injured in the army (especially if they let me serve in that battalion that catches drug dealers who try to cross the Egyptian border).
5. I could get raped literally at any given moment.

Sorry. That's kind of a weird thing to say in a birthday letter. But I guess I am weird. And so are you, *mon petit ami*. That's why we get along so well. You said it once—we're evil twins, aren't we? Besides, Liat says that my Problem has gotten much, much worse since my dad moved out last Passover. I disagree. I think she actually just feels it now that she has to spend more time with me because she feels so guilty about THE SITUATION.

Yesterday we went to buy my dress for your bar mitzvah. You're gonna absolutely love it. It is the deepest turquoise I have ever seen, and guess what? It's all made of shiny sequins, like the black dress Berta Schatz wore at the legendary concert at the Olympia in Paris, where she stood, so fine, and played the tambourine. It's gonna make me look like a giant disco ball when we dance, with my body glowing and reflecting light in all directions. And I actually think it's a shade that works well with the silver color of your suit, which I know you hate but which I still believe looks cute on you. Liat, of course, was not a fan. But naturally she bought the dress anyway because she's a spineless creature. When we got back home, I told her that if she kept being a terrible mother, I wouldn't let her come to your bar mitzvah.

You can't say that, Abbie, you have no right, she said. (She never calls me Abbie; she knows that name belongs to you and you only.)

Of course I can, Liat. You don't tell me what to do or think or say.

She cried—her usual response to confrontation. But that wasn't quite the end. I wish it were. Because then she said the craziest thing that you can possibly imagine. That was the moment that changed everything, after which nothing couldn't really be the same. Like, if you thought Liat was mad, this will literally destroy you. DESTROY YOU. Ready?

She told me, furrowing her thin black eyebrows, *Well,*

honey, it is not my fault that you are desperately in love with a boy who'll never love you back.

I didn't say a word. I knew the woman needed treatment, but I guess I didn't realize how badly. I was furious—sure, who wouldn't be—but somehow, suddenly, maybe for the first time in my life, I felt sorry for her. It was as if I'd seen her naked.

Didn't I tell you I was living with a mental case?

Later, when I got off the bus in Haifa, as I was walking from Carmel Beach station to my dad's, I texted her and blocked her number on my phone. I'd spent the entire ride working on a draft, deleting it, and starting over. *If you dare show your ugly face at his bar mitzvah you and I are done, do you hear me, it would be the end of you Liat I swear.*

In case it isn't obvious, just let me clarify: no, that useless bitch was absolutely wrong, as always, WHY WOULD I BE FUCKING IN LOVE WITH MY BEST FUCKING FRIEND ON THIS FUCKING PLANET?!?!?!?!?!?!?!?!?!

But this actually brings me to my final list, the most important one, the one I have been building up to from the moment I started writing this stupid letter so early in the morning at my dad's.

WHY IS MISTER ADAM WEIZMANN THE MOST AMAZING PERSON ON THIS EARTH (AND THE ONLY ONE WHO DOESN'T SEE IT)?

I think I'm actually gonna leave this one open, like a blank page. Not because it's empty, but because it has too many items on it. I guess that's the only way in which lists suck: they tend to have an end. But I decided, five years, three months, and twelve days ago, right after I noticed items number one and two (your smile, ridiculously tilted to the right; the way you say my name), that our list will be infinite. Yes, it is your list, too, because I'm gonna make you memorize it until you finally admit it, or at least just understand, *mon petit ami*. And I couldn't be more excited, more curious and proud, to spend an eternity writing this list with you, together, making it a little longer every day.

Yours friendfully (I swear it's a word, I checked),

XOXO,

Abbie

(Abigail)

(The best friend you've ever had and ever will)

The Shiksa

Standing on the doorstep of the house of worship, dressed in her best wool suit, Mémé shuts her eyes and tells herself she will not faint. Why is this elegant, vibrant, generally stable woman trembling with agitation on such a holy Saturday? She is excellently put together—surprisingly, perhaps, considering the pressures of this morning—and seems just as self-collected as on any other day.

The entrance to the synagogue is virtually deserted. Everybody is inside. Everything, it seems, is happening so fast in there. People whoop and chirp and cheer and clap. Even from a distance she can hear the building chant.

The air outside is cool and strangely sour. The morning news, which she habitually makes her best effort to avoid, predicted both a rainstorm and a war. Mémé has always harbored a suspicion that the two are somewhat correlated. Military operations, she has learned, rarely happen in the winter. But those that do tend to be particularly devastating for everyone involved. It is as if the cold makes men more savage. She has seen them all, the wars, in different shapes and hues. The nauseating green of years (how many years? decades, *putain*) in Lebanon. The yellow-brown of Egypt, dotted with burned tanks and corpses. She has never actually been there, no, thank goodness. She was married on the eve of her eighteenth birthday, marvelously pregnant, and barely spoke any Hebrew, so they gave her an exemption. But she has heard the stories, seen the pictures.

Now, standing motionless on Frishman Street, she thinks of rain and sirens. Mémé wonders which one will precede the other. Breathing suddenly becomes a task. But that is anything but new; it has much more to do with her own fragility than with the army or the weather.

Even from behind the wooden doors, Mémé recognizes the angelic voices—the choir that her son has hired with money that he doesn't have. Four brothers, not quadruplets but thoroughly identical. There is something oddly Catholic about this lavish celebration, so unlike her son; Jews, she knows, are taught to keep their distance from this business of extravagance. But of course she hasn't said a thing, figuring she might as well enjoy it while it lasts. This merry foursome is to accompany her grandson as he partakes in the strange *rite de passage*, ushering him into adulthood, when at long last he becomes a man.

She is half an hour late and absolutely stunning for her age. Her paprika hair—cut to the shoulders specially for the event—her suit, her suntanned skin, her whitened teeth all shine. They tell a story that the world adores about eternal youth and the wonders of persistence. She is a master story-teller, that's what everybody says. But deep inside, she recognizes that she hasn't been herself. Something isn't right with her. A certain fuzziness.

Mémé feels no urgent need to vocalize the truth, a bitter pill that she has stubbornly refused to swallow. She knows that she does not belong here, at this synagogue, or at any other synagogue, or even in this mystifying land. Although she's tried so hard to join the Chosen Folk, even officially converted—a fact that's never stopped surprising her large circle of acquaintances and friends. Why would you inflict such pain upon yourself, jumping through the infernal hoops of Judaism like a domesticated puppy at the urging of a rabbinic whip, when you know too well that you're an untamed lioness?

She has done it twice, in fact, if the first time in Salerno counts, which she strongly feels it does. How can it not, after hours of abasement at the Jewish court in Naples, the count-less Hebrew lessons, for Chrissakes, she even changed her name, and the double immersion at the mikveh (first naked in front of the female attendant; then dressed in a thin, trans-lucent robe for the pleasure of that odd trio of rabbis—she still remembers their instructions: arms loose, legs apart, gaps between the fingers, body forward, with the eyes and mouth shut, not too tightly, just like that)? But for the Chief Rabbinate of Israel, this still wasn't enough. Mémé will never be sufficient. She has descended through the nine circles of hell, only to be left at the bottom, all alone, no guide to be found, forever an intruder.

Looking back, as one does often at her age, she can't get to the root of this obsession to become a Jew. Why did she feel the need to derail her life so radically and so abruptly, when, truth be told, she had no quarrel with the Son of God, whom she'd been raised to worship? What made a nice Catholic girl—a beautiful, young shiksa, as it were, that word she loathes—whose loosely Jewish father had given her a free pass to remain a gentile want to embark on an impossible crusade to turn herself into one of them?

The answer was plain: a nice, young Jewish man. Or, to be accurate, his shtetl-fleeing, meatball-making, bridge-playing, shiksa-hating Jewish mother.

So what if Mémé forgot to take her medications earlier this morning? Perhaps *forgot* isn't the word. *Opted out* seems more appropriate. She's simply had enough of everything, and mostly of herself. The trazodone and the gabapentin— always on her person, her new best friends. The recent changes in her body: her frequent falls, her tremor, the constant stiffness of her muscles. (She used to be a proud fast walker, but these days, she can only shuffle.) Her son, disturbingly missing in action, and on his own son's most special day. Her girlfriends, who have been screening her many calls, abandoning her at an alarming rate. The clients at the jewelry store where she still works to make herself feel useful and keep the end at bay, who express the most ridiculous demands, as if the entire world economy hasn't just gone to hell. Her daughter-in-law, black-hearted, ruthless Sarah, who walks around the neighborhood calling her a slut and a slob behind her back.

Mémé instructed the taxi driver to drop her off two blocks from the synagogue, asking him to wait. Her wallet was nowhere to be found, but she would *fetch it from upstairs.*

Upstairs where? There, there. In truth, she has no clue. She rarely has a plan. Rushing past the stores on Ben Yehuda Street, closed on this early Sabbath morning, she admitted to herself that she had no intention of returning. The driver would eventually recognize his error. He shouldn't have trusted her. No one should, ever, at least not with financial matters.

But she really shouldn't think about herself today. Earlier, while whispering her routine Ave Maria still curled up in bed, she decided that this day would be all about her grandson. Her precious Adam. Her *tesoro.* She—the impossible woman that she is, the Italian renegade, the Gentile Who Fell to Earth—she will be the one to help him finally become a Jewish man.

How will she bring herself to cross the threshold? Opening the iron gate, stepping inside that secret hall of God, is a tremendous feat, Sisyphean, not meant for her. Although she has been to *beaucoup* synagogues, more than she had ever planned. She has even been to this one in particular, which never managed to appeal to her aesthetic sensibilities. Celebrating one's venture into manhood here was a family tradition—something that even her ex-husband, Adam's grandfather, may he rest in peace, did decades earlier. This was the place where her own son read his Torah portion in the 1980s in a voice that trembled like the strings of his untuned guitar, those verses that she hated to admit she couldn't understand.

Even so, today feels different. Today, her shame is back. Mémé just can't shake the feeling that if she tries to enter—which she won't, not yet—the building won't be able to contain her, will vomit her out, perhaps even explode, and she, as usual, will be the one to blame.

But she has to see her grandson. Her mamma's words then come to mind—her beloved mother, a rare jewel from an ancient world that is now lost forever. There's always a way inside, and everything can be opened up, her mamma used to tell her in Italian, until the day she ultimately lost the ability to speak, after the stroke that left her paralyzed for years, then killed her slowly, almost with politeness. If there is no door to knock on, look for a window, her mamma said. If a window is nowhere to be found, use the chimney instead. If there's no chimney (and Mémé has never seen one in five decades in the Holy Land, not even in her short stint as a secretary in Jerusalem or on her frequent trips to Nazareth), just dig a tunnel.

Has it ever been as simple as her mamma thought? Maybe Sarah was right after all? Does Mémé really make life impossible for everyone around her?

I see everything without seeing anything, she used to tell her grandson, taking on her mamma's omniscient tone.

Her Adam used to laugh, back in the days when he still

cared. He asked her in response, Mémé, what does that even mean? Is it a warning or a brag?

It's a threat, she warned him. Your Mémé's still around, you know. I'm always watching you. I'm always there.

And there she is, outside the house of worship, dressed in her best wool suit, which she bought and hemmed and dry-cleaned with the remnants of her most recent paycheck. Already failing to deliver on her promise. Alive to everything around her, even the little ladybug that's started climbing up the thin blue veins that ornament her scrawny calf. Mémé reaches down with her index finger, inviting the beetle to hop on it. The ladybug complies. It zigzags across the small hills of her crumpled finger and ventures straight into her palm, moving back and forth in tiny circles. Mémé smiles; it tickles.

Then, flicking the ladybug and watching it float in midair, she understands: her mamma, as always—or at least on most occasions—was correct. There *is* a window. A huge one, on the right side of the building, behind a thicket of fig trees and tangled shrubs. Bright, colorful, and arched, at odds with the largely unembellished nature of the synagogue, more fitting to a mosque or even, God forbid, a church.

Yes, there is a window. And it is whispering her Christian name, which she left behind in Italy. The one they made her cast aside when her papa dragged her to get her Israeli passport in Jerusalem. Her tears were bitter, like black pepper, she remembers. Don't cry, *tesoro*, her papa whispered as they left the Ministry of the Interior, hand in hand, marching down the long, wide street. Pretend you were a caterpillar, a beautiful, Neapolitan caterpillar that has shed its skin and turned into a butterfly. Now you can fly, my darling dear. She said nothing; her lips were stitched together. If she felt like anything back then, it was a moth, at best.

What Mémé really is, she's come to realize, is a fox, an expert sneak. She used to break out of her parents' building in Salerno, where her mamma had grown up, where she met her papa after he fled his village in the Soviet Union when the Nazis started their invasion. Mémé was born there, in Salerno, one month after an impromptu wedding, a Judeo-Christian union none of their neighbors had been able to anticipate or understand. A little redhead, slipping out to lick pistachio ice cream at the port and gaze at seagulls by herself.

When she was ten, they moved to Israel against her will because her father got a governmental post. She always thought he was a spy but never found hard evidence. Every time she could, she snuck out of the Collège des Sœurs de Jaffa, her Catholic school for girls, where the nuns would only let her choose between French and Latin, between Jacques le Juste and Jacques de Zébédée. She remembers the tamarind trees in the courtyard, her light blue uniform with its white collar, the French embroidery lessons with Madame Agnès. At dusk, Mémé would run barefoot down Yefet Street and up the stairs of the Armenian monastery, climbing all the way to the roof to watch the day die on Andromeda's Rock. She loved the chanting of the muezzin, the lulling rustle of the waves. Sometimes she would be up there with a lover, infatuated, screaming corny phrases from Petula Clark—*la nuit ne finira donc pas, prends mon cœur si tu veux*—and holding hands.

Later on, but not too much—she married at eighteen, dodging the military service, something that Adam couldn't understand—she crawled out of her ex-husband's bed. The father of her only son. The man whose jealous rages taught her how to tiptoe, whose passion was like sulfuric acid, corroding everything that it encountered, including her.

Then, after they finally got divorced on what she liked to call her Independence Day, after he vowed to kill her and himself, Mémé fled a host of other beds, usually in posh hotel rooms, where men with ample chest hair pronounced her name in foreign accents—French, Moroccan, British, Russian, Japanese—and promised her a brand-new life elsewhere. If breaking free from men were an Olympic sport, she used to tell her friends when she was tipsy, she would most definitely win the gold.

Now, this synagogue. A brutalist, repellent monster—an old epitome of Bauhaus, as tour guides and travel agents falsely tell the world—made of bigotry and gray cement. She had been officially barred from inviting anyone to escort her into this monster's maw. Not even Gabrielle, her closest friend, who has known Adam almost since birth, has loved him like a grandson, has taught him how to sew and sing the "Marseillaise."

We'd like to keep it *intimate*, Sarah said, savoring the sweetness of the opportunity to twist the dagger in Mémé's heart. Mémé doesn't need to step inside the synagogue to understand that was a blatant lie. There are at least a hundred people in attendance. A hundred souls—probably many more if you count the dead, which Mémé always does—dressed in their finest. Not a single one for her.

In fact, there was one friend they had allowed her to invite: Berta Schatz, the fabled singer, who has been her pal since they first crossed paths sometime in the seventies. They all admired Berta—her beauty and her talent were unparalleled—but Adam more than everyone combined. He was obsessed. To most people, his adoration was a riddle. Berta had stopped being a household name back in the eighties and hadn't really been around, although her songs were still played on the radio every now and then.

Sarah was disturbed, offended, even. Why would he care so much about an old lady who barely leaves her bedroom, let alone sings? What's wrong with movie stars and soccer players? Mémé knew better than try to argue or explain. She recognized there was no weapon she could use against Sarah's arsenal of prejudices in disguise, her brand of faux liberalism that has become the plague of Tel Aviv and its quaint suburbs.

When Mémé was young, folks were radical. Even she dabbled a bit, although she always thought that politics were wildly overrated. Though it may seem unthinkable today, she drove to Gaza and Ramallah several times in the pre-Oslo years. One of her close friends used to broadcast radio shows about peace and coexistence from a ship in the middle of the sea, against the law. Things were happening; there was a throbbing sense of progress. People came out, in the squares and on the streets. Even the Arabs were around, including several of her peers at the Collège des Sœurs. They weren't everywhere, of course, but one could *see* them. There were no walls, and if there were, they were less visible, more pliant. It's not as if there weren't wars; there were, horrific ones. Mémé remembers how she had to cover every single window in her small apartment with black tape so that they wouldn't shatter during bombings. Or how she stumbled, pregnant, while running to the municipal shelter down the block during the Six-Day War. Those were the days.

Back then, the great figures of state—Dayan, Golda, even Begin, whom she could never stand—were still alive and kicking. They had something real to offer, even to a shiksa like herself. Or so she thought. Now they're all gone; their vision, pride, and passion have faded with them. Life in Israel, she is convinced, has become too comfortable, and comfort breeds complacency. One too many cappuccinos on the boulevard can make one blind. Now the Israelis clung to words, so many words. Hollow ones, untranslatable, perverse. Words meant to hide more than reveal the world around them. Mémé has always hated words. Sometimes she wishes she could find a way to rid herself of the cacophony of language altogether. The country where she's made her home is now a twilight zone. The generation has become degenerate.

Although she thinks she understands her grandson. At least she tries to, even when she struggles. Has he ever met Berta? She isn't sure. Not that she recalls. It doesn't really matter. Because for Adam, Berta is a myth. A figment of his fiery imagination. What she symbolizes, Mémé can't quite tell. Somehow, she stirs something in Adam's soul. To be fair, it doesn't take a lot; he's always been easily inspired, a little connoisseur who mistakes the world for a museum. He was the only boy she knew who could recite the textbook definition of Cubism before he learned to read. Perhaps it was her fault. After all, when he was small, she was the one who showed him Monet's *Nymphéas* at the Orangerie, took him to the circus when it came to town, and told him tales about Baudelaire and Mallarmé.

One day, in middle school, when he was asked to write something about a hero of his choosing, he told her he had entertained the thought of using Berta as his subject. Mémé laughed. At first, she thought it was one of his jokes, which always baffled her. His slanted eyebrows made it clear that he was serious.

Well, is there anything that strikes you as heroic about Berta? Mémé asked her grandson, genuinely curious.

Adam was adamant. What do you mean? he said. It's everything, her whole existence. She came here as an outcast, all alone, so poor, just to live on some kibbutz. Then she moved to Tel Aviv because she wanted to fulfill her dream and be a modern dancer. Which she kind of did, I guess, against all odds. She was a singer, which I think is even better. And she barely spoke the language! And she never even tried to hide her accent. (He was right; Berta wore her accent on her sleeve, with elegance, in a time when people with the faintest smell of foreignness were seen as existential threats.) There was that thing I read about online—they said her husband hit her so hard and so often that she had to run away.

Mémé had tried to obfuscate the details. Adam was too young, too sheltered. Sometimes he reminded her of herself when she was his age. No wonder people often thought she was his mother. Mémé was proud to be the source of his romanticism. There was so much he didn't—shouldn't— know. Not yet.

But it was true: even in middle school, the boy knew his stuff when it came to research. Berta had been terribly abused. Her husband was a drunk. And Berta was too kind, always incredibly forgiving. At last, after years of turbulence and terror, she left him. One night, with no warning, she emerged from a taxi on Mémé's doorstep, schlepping two purple suitcases. There were no bruises on her body and no tears in her eyes, but her face—proud, terrified, solemn—spoke for her.

Mémé made a bed for Berta and boiled a *macchinetta* and called her travel agent, purchasing three plane tickets in six installments. Soon enough, Berta was gone. She left the country with her kids, flying back to Philadelphia, where she'd been born. They kept in touch, sending each other birthday cards and lengthy letters. Mémé struggled to decipher Berta's scrawly cursive, but she did her best. Berta married an American who died a few years later in a helicopter accident. When Berta's parents passed, she returned to Israel in secret and kept her head down as much as she was able to. She barely made public appearances and was a notorious interview refusenik, living on royalties and National Insurance payments. Mémé, already divorced at that point in her life, learned from her pal's misfortunes and vowed never to remarry, a pledge that she has gladly kept.

Inside the synagogue, someone is speaking stridently, sawing the air with his plump hands. She sees his silhouette, illuminated, like in a shadow play. Mémé takes a few steps toward the window, attempting to discern a little more than necks and outlines. At first, she thinks the speaker is their gray-haired family friend who used to offer her cash to make love to him until he realized there was no buying her. What was his name again? Then she recalls; he died last spring. Gone in less than four months. Lung cancer.

Perhaps it is that rabbi who dared tell Adam that, according to the scriptures, sexual inverts were to be stoned to death. That motherfucking piece of crap.

Oh, you and your short fuse again, her son said, predictably defending his messianic friend. Rabbi Ginsberg was just stating a fact.

And after all, he wasn't wrong; even a gentile like herself knew that the Torah had little fondness for the fairies. But what that fundamentalist had said, she still believes, caused her grandson to retreat into his shell—to refuse to speak or eat for two whole days—and that, to her, is a sin beyond forgiveness.

Peering through the great, arched window, still in hiding, Mémé recognizes that the shadow cannot be the rabbi's. The man, whose head she still struggles to see through the abundant vegetation, is wearing a loose tank top of some kind. He's muscular, perhaps a soldier on vacation. No, it's not the rabbi then. If she saw him, though, she surely wouldn't be able to control herself. She would break every single bone in that consecrated body. How dare he cause her grandson pain?

Just as she thinks she has finally caught a glimpse of Adam's head as he climbs to the podium, agitated, something on the street captures her attention. Someone. The past.

An extraordinary woman is walking by, undisturbed, dressed in a blue long-sleeve dress. Recently, Mémé has been struggling with faces, histories, and names (sometimes, on particularly foggy mornings, she worries that she might forget her own). But in this case, she doesn't have to ask herself where she has seen this woman.

Her name is Liliana, but everybody used to call her Lily, even the most heartless of the nuns. Her family had also moved to Israel from Italy, but Lily was originally from the north, which, to a *terrona* like Mémé, was basically another country. Mémé and Lily overlapped at the Collège des Sœurs for a year. Lily was the only one in that repressive institution who could see Mémé as more than just an odd bird. The two of them baffled everyone at the Collège, two foreign elements, uniquely stubborn in their strangeness. Their sweet alliance ended much sooner than they'd hoped, cut short by the sorry circumstances of their lives, but mostly by the wrath of Lily's father.

Lily! Mémé yells, and then again, and even louder this time, It's Maria! *Sono io!* You are back!

Seized by a sudden urgency, as if her oldest living friend is about to sink into oblivion, Mémé starts running up the street. She yanks the shoulder of the woman she hasn't seen in decades. And there she is in front of her, Lily Avallone.

Even after all this time, Lily's face is luminous—not a wrinkle to be seen—and just as kind as Mémé has remembered. A wave of unease washes over Lily's eyes. She seems preoccupied. Is it the sight of Mémé's evident decline that rattles her? She must have married, maybe even twice, although Mémé can identify no ring. She must have raised her children somewhere near the coast, as she had always planned. She must have kept devising sonnets, perhaps addressed to others, maybe even published—under a pseudonym, if at all, for Mémé has sought her name in the Italian papers every now and then.

Does Lily still play the piano with one hand and her eyes closed? Does she still bite her bottom lip every time she's faced with a math problem, however simple? Does she ever think of Mémé on sleepless nights or early mornings, like the ones they used to share? How come she looks entirely unchanged?

Mémé knows that, in the interim, she herself has turned into a different person. The years have drained her, squashed her, altered something fundamental in her essence, something that she couldn't name. Her disaster of an ex-husband, may he rest in peace, whom she married and divorced sixteen miserable months later. Their myriad debts. Her later years in Italy, where she was shocked to recognize she had become a stranger even in her motherland. Her business trips to India and France, back when she thought she could break into the fashion world. Her love affairs, always consisting of too little love. The plastic surgeries that emptied each of her many bank accounts, and which she stubbornly denies. Her poor, dear son, Yishai, God help his soul. His illness that she's never really found the time or language to address. Her long-dead parents, who left her nothing but that old apartment in Salerno, which she lost. Their ghosts, with whom she sleeps and wakes. And Sarah, so perpetually hostile, who despises her because, deep down, she recognizes that their tendencies—to self-preserve and self-mythologize—are just the same.

Now this woman, her old friend, adorable on Frishman Street. Astonishingly young. No longer absent. Like a figure from the underworld, outside of time; a statue in an old museum. Like a tourist from another land. Why has she never written, never called? What seas has she traversed over almost half a century? Is the Collège des Sœurs still standing as it was when they were twelve and the world was a forbidden piece of the head nun's apple cake?

Mémé feels a pounding urge to speak, to reminisce about the good old days, which were actually good, she is convinced, not just in a nostalgic way. Lily stares at her, refusing to grant any sign of recognition. Is she even really there?

It dawns on Mémé: next to Lily, overshadowed by her radiance, stands a man, sturdy and impatient. They have been walking down the street together. Her son? A husband?

Maybe just a friend? He grabs the woman by the arm and pulls her toward him.

Hey, Mémé wants to shout. Hey, *monsieur*, easy there.

Come on, the man says. This lady is bananas. Let's go, babe.

But Lily doesn't care to look at him. Her eyes are fixed on Mémé.

Come on. The man gives Lily's arm another pull. We're going.

Where?

Maybe Mémé can articulate the buried passions she's been trying to unravel. Perhaps there is a term she can retrieve, perhaps in French. But an acute pain pierces her chest from inside, deriding her, emptying her mind, forcing her to bend and clutch her knees. Her lungs have never been so small. And once again, her body breaks.

When she manages to rise, she tries to catch her breath. How much time has even passed? The woman and the man are gone. Mémé looks around. When did she stop being a girl?

She feels a soft pat on her shoulder. Ma'am, a pregnant woman says. Is everything okay?

Mémé bows, unable to make words of her thoughts. The world is silent, like a television screen on mute.

She mutters something. The woman nods and smiles, then leaves. Gingerly, as if walking a tightrope, Mémé starts to make her way back to the synagogue. Her grandson needs her. She hears his voice, which hasn't broken yet. Mémé tries to smile for him, her Adam, humming an Italian song she used to love, whose lyrics she cannot remember for the life of her.

She thinks, There is no other time than now.

She thinks, Why am I always tardy?

She thinks, Today I will be brave.

Outside the house of worship that was never hers, as she listens to the sweet drone of her grandson's off-key voice blend with the song that spills out of her mouth, Mémé shuts her eyes and reaches for the gate.

Mrs. Weizmann

Why on earth did they bring the lilacs, god, when she had asked literally three hundred times for roses, she couldn't have been clearer on that point, and now the centerpieces look like someone sacked some Lithuanian ghetto, and that's it, *kaput*, nine months of labor down the drain.

The smell of cinnamon kebabs and deep-fried chicken assails her nostrils as she climbs the stairs, holding the hem of her red silk dress in one hand and in the other a glass of chardonnay—her third—like a drunken Cinderella, sans pumpkin carriage, no fairy godmother to be seen, alas, even though, like Cinderella's, hers is an orphan story, but she is not quite sure about the happy-ending bit, she will have to make sure that the entrées are out by seven, seven thirty at the latest, people are impatient, useless, tasteless, untrustworthy, nothing ever comes into existence in this world unless she makes it happen.

What a blast, a fete, she has never felt so vital, so attuned to the universe and its mysterious ways, fixing her hair, fine-tuning her makeup, running her chubby, sweaty fingers down her dress, traversing the still-deserted dance floor with the determination of a drill sergeant. Soon it will be populated with family and friends, who will flood the banquet hall with their hugs and dance moves, people Adam loves and she despises; or people he had asked her not to invite but she did anyway, secretly, out of pity or of obligation; or people that she actually quite likes and Adam has no strong feelings about because he's so accommodating, nothing like herself or like her loser husband, Adam's father, who can't even get along with his imaginary friends, a lunatic in a polyester suit, a scam with legs. She is by no means a believer, but she prays to god he will respect her stipulation and won't grace them tonight with the misfortune of his presence.

Because—she reckoned, sadly, far too late—her husband was another confirmation of her long-standing suspicion that despite some cunningly misleading features (flat chests, fast metabolism, greater upper-body strength)—despite their I'll fix the car and I'll unblock the sink and I'll take the kid to see a soccer match on Saturday and I and I and I and I and honey why don't you put on some coffee in the meantime—at the very root of their existence, men are weak. Sheep in wolves' clothing. False prophets of fabricated confidence trained by our culture to speak their prophecies in deep, low, reassuring voices. They've learned to wear black ties and formal trousers just so they can hide the fact that beneath their suits their underwear is soaking wet.

She wanted him to prove her wrong. She thought he would, when he nodded at the trattoria where he took her on their first date, as she carefully unwove the fine threads of her past, already oversharing twenty minutes into their conversation, narrating her personal *Les Misérables* and grinding Parmesan on her spaghetti Bolognese. She told Yishai about the nights in cramped hospital rooms in Jerusalem with her dying mother and early mornings cleaning stairwells and apartments as an undergraduate. He nodded and listened and murmured that's crazy and I'm sorry like several had done before, and his good eyes opened wide, but something about him—what was it?—something about him made her say, well, maybe this time it is different. It was shortly after her friend Orly told her he was a gifted basketball player and a passionate lover, a future lawyer, a notorious troublemaker, but, deep inside, a true feminist (you know, one of those *very* modern men).

A true feminist. Ha. Like labeling Diet Coke a superfood. Feminist men belong to that questionable category of twenty-first-century oxymorons, part of that postmodern mythology that she despises, along with monogamous homosexuals, liberal Arabs, and a Jewish-loving Germany, a virtual reality that exists only within the shrinking confines of cafés in downtown Tel Aviv and liberal arts colleges in rural Massachusetts.

Waiters and waitresses in suits crisscross the hall in some imagined hurry, rushing to deliver plates and glasses to invisible guests, lighting candles, unrolling white tablecloths on tall, round tables, distributing tiny challahs, running after her and crying Mrs. Weizmann, Mrs. Weizmann, as if British Mandate Palestine has made a one-night comeback, murmuring good evening and hello into the void. As she marches past the chocolate fountain, back and forth, possessed, she just can't shake the feeling that something dreadful is about to happen, perhaps because of the announcer on the morning news who said the words to which she'd grown so painfully accustomed—our forces are gathering around the border—and she immediately thought of her nephew Ben, poor thing, who must be peeing his pants at just the thought of an invasion, and once again she smells the stench of bonfire and mud, which has always been, for her, the harbinger of military operations. Although they're peace-seeking people, all of them, or at least most, yes, despite everything people say about them throughout the entire world, which, as every sane person knows but only the truly decent are willing to admit even in 2009, comes down to the old antisemitic libels.

But they ought to celebrate tonight. Celebrating is a mitzvah, not a sin. To be sure, she knows nothing—when it comes to Judaism, she is as ignorant as an empty jar of pickles. Willingly so, of course; religion is a cult, it's driven far too many people in her life berserk, but she tries, like most people, or some, to be a better person, to sublimate herself, to crawl out of her angst as if it were a swamp, to peel off years of poverty and orphanhood and disappointments—terror attacks, lost jobs, marital despair. She has not flinched, not even once, not even for a moment, although her life has been a slasher film at times, but she's survived, she's a survivor, and now she is determined, she has decided that this night would be one to remember, even if those fucking roses still haven't arrived—and never will, no need to pretend, the florist must have misremembered, she will have to find forgiveness in her heart, for him and for all other fellow beings in this world— she will make her son happy at all costs, even if that means putting aside her ego (what her husband calls her egomania), or talking amicably to people she would rather drown in an acid bath, or forgetting all about her marriage, the recession, her unemployment (what her sister calls the Unbearable Unemployability of the Literary Scholar), the impending storm, the neighbors' renovations every day from dawn to dusk, the bouncing checks, the never-ending story known as her doctoral dissertation (what her adviser calls *Virginia Woolf and the Impossibility of F(r)iction*), the friends who've disappeared, the chin hair, the prospect of alcoholism, all— and endlessly more—a price that she would be thrilled to pay if she could only make her son, for one time in his life, relax.

It bothers her that he has never really told her. Nor has he told his father, by the way, or any of his friends. Not even Abigail. At least not to her knowledge. Of course she knows. Mothers cannot help but know. But she needs him to say it himself. She wants him to do it in accordance with proto- col. She likes things to be explicitly stated, firmly sealed, with no room for close readings and further interpretations. She wants her share of deep sighs and long pauses, of Mom and Dad, I have something to tell you, of when did you find out and why didn't you say and how long have you known and was I a bad mother, not in the sense of *Crime and Punishment*, god no, you know I'm not one for Dostoyevsky, and besides I'm liberal to the bone, just in the sense of, well, why didn't you say, did you not know I'd be there for you, always have been, always will be, always, always, even if you rape and murder, which I really hope you don't? I think I've given you a pretty decent education, when you were six you jumped onto the couch and said I was your best friend, god, is that no longer true, are you uncomfortable, tell me the truth, my treasure, it's all right, you can talk to me, you know, I feel as if I gave birth and then blinked and somehow you became a man.

She has so many questions burning in her brain. But there's no rush, not today. They still have time. Some people die at ninety, even a hundred these days. And they are healthy, *toi toi toi*, both of them. They say that only at thirteen do you start to see your parents as real people, and suddenly they're flawed, well-rounded characters—her own mother did not live long enough to enjoy that privilege.

And this evening is indeed so very special, she's wanted it to be, for him, her boy, her Adam, and also for herself. She trades her empty glass for yet another chardonnay, the green-eyed waiter smiles at her, he seems familiar, maybe a student, she reciprocates and nods and heads down to the entrance, to schmooze, to greet the early birds who for whatever reason dared show up a full twenty minutes before the time printed in large, bold letters on their invitations. She walks, exhausted but somehow ebullient, she looks for a familiar face, too bad, all she can see now is her own reflection, heinous, ancient, in different hues and textures—the glasses, ceiling, bottles, windows, floor, why so many golden mirrors everywhere—she shuts her eyes and listens to the music, an annoyingly familiar song she can't identify, she knew she shouldn't have skimped on the DJ, Daddy, if that's even his name, he was the best they could afford, and the sour lady at the bank said they'd reached their loan ceiling, so they didn't have a choice, oh, what a shame; she swallows, fast-forwarding the evening in her head: first appetizers, finger food, and cocktails, then Adam's much-anticipated entrance just as they've rehearsed—lights, fireworks, balloons, confetti, the carrot cake he loves with the picture from his sixth grade concert that he hates, Ch-Ch-Ch-Ch-Changes by Bowie blasts the hall, Time may change me, but I can't trace—then entrées, finally, if people haven't died of famine by then, a dance party for as long as the young can last, but under no circumstances longer than an hour, then speeches, including her own, which she has still yet to compose, writing has become a torture, it has been weeks since she last saw her desk, then his duet with the old singer from the sixties that he loves, that quirky boy of hers, and afterward, desserts (tragically, all pareve, thanks to her dopey husband), a digestif—then home in a taxi, floating on a cloud of soft intoxication, to count the checks in bed and calculate the damage.

One thing is clear: if she survives this evening, she will surely live through anything, from another Holocaust to the horrors of old age. The secret is to smile, smile hard, smile until her cheeks begin to hurt, until she can't quite breathe, she has got to laugh and chat and sing out loud, even the silly Spanish songs she hates, and dance, and drink herself into marvelous oblivion, and, most important, look better than her sister, so help her god, she will do anything to make this evening beautiful and unforgettable, for him and for herself, jeez, what a thrill to be a mother.

Daddy: An Interlude

"One, two ... Eh ... One, one ... Liko, can you turn it down a little over there? Ladies and gentlemen, thank you all for sharing this beautiful, BEAUTI-FUL evening with the Weizmanns. We will begin shortly, no more than twenty minutes, our sincerest apologies if you've been waiting. We've been dealing with some technical difficulties on our end. Nothing you should be concerned about, of course. The bar mitzvah boy is, as you can imagine, quite excited. After all, it doesn't happen every day that you become a man. But hopefully, yes, very soon all will be resolved, and we'll be able to embark on the adventure of this evening. In the meantime, please enjoy the appetizers, our HORS D'OEUVRES, as they say, courtesy of the authentic Elqame restaurant in Yafia village. You must've read about them in *Haaretz*, there was a big story about Chef Hussam's SAINTLY work. I am telling you, that man—I had the honor of meeting him earlier, a thoroughly modern person, a true mensch. He has plenty of delicacies in store for us, including—take my word for it—his famous testicles, sheep testicles, I mean, caramelized and roasted in his traditionally operated oven, which dates back to the old days of the Ottomans, served with a yummy sauce of artichoke-tahini . . ."

Daddy takes another sip of beer. Whoever was in charge of the design of this event went too hard on the gold; every corner of the banquet hall is glittering. The few guests who have already arrived—no more than forty, forty-five at most—applaud politely, although it's clear that they don't give a damn. They drink and chuckle, making hushed comments they hope nobody hears. They say hello to someone they think they haven't seen in years, even though they have, of course; the someone has just undergone a hair transplant in Turkey, which rendered him unrecognizable. They speak. How are you (bitch), how is your mother (the dirty hag), how is work going (I wish you bankruptcy and illness). They tap a waiter's shoulder, snatch an appetizer, then another, gulping them down, making sure that no one witnesses the hour of their greed.

Soon they will be clustered around tables and in corners, taking on their designated roles. First the crones—pals of the grandmother, who looks much younger than he would have expected, and whose extravagant white 1980s suit suggests this may be her own bat mitzvah. All laughing far too loudly, showing off their new dentures, each with her respective pearl necklace and flea-infested scarf. Shrouded in a cloud of citrus perfume that upsets Daddy's stomach even from a distance.

Then the buddies of the father, who is still yet to arrive, dressed in cargo shorts and button-downs, lightly stained with oil and coffee, looking like they're just about to go out fishing. A true disgrace to their sex, no sense of style; men will be men. And the kids—an unfortunate necessity at parties.

Among the little devils, too many waiters of varied ethnic minorities, huffing and puffing, poor servants of Capital, just like himself. Then, finally, a host of what he likes to call appendices: people whose presence at the party is like that of carrots in a salad—harmless, unobtrusive. They are his favorites; he's seen them at festivities of every kind, from funerals to weddings.

"Hey, kids, hey, I'm sorry, just a few steps back now, please, I'm asking you, hey, what the— don't you push me, and don't get near the station either, I don't wanna see your little faces here, not now and not at all this evening. Do you hear me? Do you understand? HEY, I'm not kidding here, okay, take three steps back now, please, yes, that's it, thanks, and don't come near us, we gotta focus here, we're working, have I not been clear on that? Just beat it."

He wouldn't have been here if that wedding in Ashkelon hadn't been called off. Too bad. The menu was much more appetizing than this pseudo-liberal feast whose only purpose is to make the guests feel more enlightened. And the bride in Ashkelon seemed *muy caliente*. He'd love to dip his biscuit into that steaming teacup. But he understands. You'd have to be completely nuts to get married near the border—or anywhere, really—these days. He won't charge the young couple. No way. He's a good guy. Those fucking Arabs can't give them a break. Gaza has been heating up, as always. Not a single day of peace.

"Ladies and gentlemen, ladies and—okay, come on now, Liko, be sharp, turn it up a little there, no, NO, not that knob, I'll just come and do it, dumbass, come on, what is going on with you, you're not with me today, you better get a grip or I will—YES, well, friends, before we start, one critical request, if I may. I have been doing this for years, so I respectfully ask, please, DON'T approach us with requests for songs. You see, I know we're all very excited, but the lineup has been carefully selected by your humble servant, Daddy the DJ, Daddy Cool. So, while we're sure that you all have outstanding taste in music, we won't be able to accommodate your wonderful requests tonight. Yes, that's the policy, my friends, I'm sorry. And I am warning you, it will be enforced with a strong hand and an outstretched arm, my apologies."

The truth is that Daddy hates these people and he hates their ways. Their lavishness. The shamelessness of their existence. Even the look on their remodeled faces when they ask if he can play "Yes Sir, I Can Boogie" or "The Ketchup Song" just one more time, *s'il vous plaît*. Catering to their demands, enacting their fantasies like this has made him sick—literally bedridden. Sometimes just the thought of getting out of bed feels like a struggle. Sometimes he finds himself sitting in his Bar-mobile (or Bat-mobile, if the birthday boy's a girl) and wishing he could drive it off a cliff.

But he doesn't have a choice. Good acting gigs are impossible to come by these days. And since that cereal ad that was a hit two years ago—*YEAH, I'M A SUCKER FOR THE HONEYSUCKLE, FOLKS*—he hasn't had much luck with casting directors. Nor with the ladies, to be honest. They all say his face has become too recognizable, too *branded*. He understands. Who wants to hire (or be penetrated by) the guy who tries to sell you diabetes in a box every night between *Survivor: All-Stars* and reruns of *Grey's Anatomy*? And his mother mandated that he vacate her basement in Afula by the end of March. So here he is, wearing his high school baseball cap and a Hawaiian shirt he hasn't washed in ages, giving a four-hour blow job to the Israeli bourgeoisie.

"SO, what do we have on tonight? Well, I'm a firm believer in the power of suspense, but I will say we are about to share a truly UNFORGETTABLE soiree. My sources tell me there's a slideshow in the works, terrific music, delicious food, as well as speeches by family and friends that will stir your soul and make you weep . . ."

Daddy remembers one blind date, a while ago, with a bespectacled lady who started off their dinner at Peking Duck by asking about the origin of his strange stage name. *Don't you think it is a little, how to put it,* patriarchal *on your end? Trying to assert your masculinity like that?*

On most occasions, speech is not one of his problems. His best friend, Rami, diagnosed him with a hopeless case of verbal diarrhea. But that lady really left him dumbstruck. *Sugar,* he meant to say, *I wouldn't overthink it, it was a pure business decision, they said Aviel Leibowitz was no name for* a DJ, so I just translated, to give it a little international flair, you know, Aviel, Daddy, baby doll, what does it matter, we're all Jews here, like a big bag of kosher M&M's, we might look different, but we taste the same.

Of course the real reason is completely different. But he didn't feel like he could share it with the lady. Maybe that was because of those same vulnerability problems she insisted that he had two weeks later when she dumped him.

It was, as always, that bastard Rami who'd taught Daddy the trick. Whenever he was short on cash, with no events in sight, he would drop by his ATM of choice: Haemek Hospital, building number three, fourth door on the right. There, Dr. Baum, director of the sperm bank, would turn a blind eye to Daddy's age—well outside the limit—and offer him two hundred shekels for his secret sauce. At this point, he probably has dozens of offspring scattered all around the country, ignorant of his existence. He likes to think of himself as Jack the Ripper, but upside down. A serial life-giver with the most potent weapon of all: a little spritz.

"Ladies and gentlemen, earlier today, our boy recited his Torah portion at the beautiful Beit El Synagogue. The critics are raving, and I hear that someone has been already nominated for a Grammy, so Lady Gaga, if you're there, beware . . .

"But if you missed his earlier performance, like me, have no fear. Tonight, Adam Weizmann will re-create his musical success with our mystery guest of honor—WHO IS SHE? I have been strictly prohibited from disclosing this top secret information. I swear to God; I couldn't even tell that Mossad agent who came up to me earlier and said the national security of our little country depended on it. All I can say is that she's a fantastic singer whose work is engraved in our collective consciousness, a woman we all know and love, even though some of us may have forgotten, one of our most fundamental cultural assets. So, we'll talk again soon, VERY soon, stay tuned, and in the meantime, HAVE A BALL, my buddies."

Now he sees her: the boy's mother, dressed in pathetic red. Waving hysterically at him, as if choking on the olive pit in her martini. What does she want, the witch? Her anguish overflows; it smells like garbage. It must've been some years since she last had a shag. She's asking him to turn the music down. That he can do, now that he's taken over his nephew Liko's spot. How did he let his sister talk him into hiring that bonehead? He didn't even need a right-hand man.

The mother doubles down; she yells something at Daddy like some kind of meshuggener. What's the rush? They still have at least a dozen songs until the speeches, don't they? One of these days she'll turn into a Botox junkie like her friends, thinking it'll make her sexy, which it won't. She walks around the dance floor like a peacock with a broken tail. Look at her, look. And there's no stopping her, no, Houston, the rocket has been launched, and we have a problem, because now she staggers onstage and clears her throat and speaks.

❧

"Can I get everyone's attention? Yes, put down that little fork of yours there, Tikvah, and listen to me now. Don't worry, yes, the shish kebab can wait, my dear.

"Wow . . . Okay. So now I understand why they told me to write something in advance. Could you turn that spotlight down a little, Daddy? Cheers.

"So we're all here . . . for you . . . my Adam. Treasure. On this very special day. And it is, indeed, so very special, as they say. I wanted it to be. I know how much it means to you, how long you have been waiting for it, how long we've all been . . . And now it's here, and we're all so very happy, and so grateful to be here—where is he, my boy? Oh, there he is, cuckoo—we're all so very proud and thrilled to see you grow, becoming this kind, generous, handsome human being.

"You know, my love, I was thinking the other day. My mother—your grandma, who unfortunately never met you but who would have been so proud of the wonder that you are—my mother died, as you know, when I was just about your age. And my father was never really there. Yes, yes. Daddy issues, mommy issues . . . The whole shebang. Absolutely.

"I celebrated my bat mitzvah trying to salvage a chocolate bar that was melting in my pocket on the 480 bus line to Jerusalem, on my way to visit my mother in Hadassah Hospital. The good old oncology department. How's that for a party, heh?

"Okay, now, time jump, sorry, time jump, about twenty years later. You and I on our weekly grocery store run. You are sitting in the shopping cart—you must have been seven or eight—eating grapes out of the box, even though you know I say you never should because they're unwashed and full of pesticides and besides we haven't even paid yet, so it's technically theft. Suddenly you look at me like the fish in that Bishop poem, your eyes so much larger than mine, yes, like that fish, and you ask me, 'Do you ever regret having me?'

"I am shocked. I feel like I can die right there, between the dairy section and the bread. And I don't want to sound too morbid—you were such an easy child, and I was always so terrified of fucking you up in one way or another, despite what my beloved sister likes to say—so I just mutter, 'Of course not, what are you talking about, sweetheart?' And I stop the cart and look you in the eyes and say, 'Never. Do you hear me? Never.' And then I kiss you on the mouth, and you wipe my kiss off with disgust, as you still do to this very day.

"But what I'm dying to tell you—and I can't, because you're still a kid, even though you talk and walk around the world like an adult—I'm dying to tell you about that atrocious bus ride to Jerusalem. And how I made a promise to myself—more of a vow, perhaps—that I would have kids. Lots. I wanted my own version of a Brady Bunch—you probably don't even know what that means—you know, like the ultra-Orthodox, I mean, so many kids that I'll start to forget their names. And when I have my kids, I'll do everything I can to protect them from this world. That's essentially what I've been doing since that day, or rather since the day when you were born, which wasn't that much later, to be frank—I was a young, hip mother, as some of you here know, or as you can all just tell by the way I look this evening . . .

"So I want to use this opportunity, now that you're no longer a kid, to tell you the truth, my Adam: I can't.

"Life screws you, honey. Over and over, from every possible direction. And there's nothing I can really do about that. Sometimes it's a downpour of shit, all of a sudden, out of nowhere. So, sooner or later, you learn that you don't really have a choice but open your arms wide and, as the Arabs say, just sing to it. And often, it's much more painful than you think.

"I didn't plan to drop my dissertation halfway through, but I had no parents and I had a baby who was—is—dearer to me than anything else on this earth. I didn't plan to gain nine kilos. I didn't plan to leave your father, that lovely man, after so many long years of marriage. Or to talk about it here, at your bar mitzvah. If you'd asked even a week ago, I would have said I'd come to terms with my fate of life with a loony.

"But we'll figure it out. Surely. We'll survive, right? We're survivors. I mean, it's not as if we broke the bank on this party. Which we absolutely did. Oh, well.

"Besides, monogamy's a bitch, as I always . . .

"Where did he . . .

"Okay. I'm sorry, I think I might have . . .

"Wow. Sorry. Shit.

"I'm sorry.

"Where did my Adam go?

"Daddy, are you there? Will you play something happy?"

Tikkun

Two or three days after she gave birth—the happiest day of my entire life—she dropped you on the floor. Like you'd drop a bundle of dirty underwear or socks. Just dropped you on the floor. *Paf. Bam.*

I couldn't breathe, as if there was a stone stuck in my throat. I tried to say something, to scream, but I couldn't even swallow. *Paf.* Mindlessly. Like that.

My mouth was dry. It felt like someone sucked the air out of my brain with a vacuum cleaner. I ran straight to the kitchen, trying to wash my terror down with water. I realized I had to be fast. You didn't cry. Your mouth was shut, your eyes wide open. And when I looked at you, you smiled. You didn't laugh. There was some kind of novelty to it. Suddenly, there was a *why* to my existence.

That was probably one of the only times you've ever seen your old man cry, big boy. There's no way you remember that.

Yes, we were good, your mom and I. I think. When we

were young (too young!), some even said we were the best. She wanted you more than anything. Today I can admit I didn't. She used to say that parenthood would help us understand ourselves, which I always found bizarre. But she was right. Your presence was enlightening; it helped me see the world more clearly. We got married in the spring, during the Gulf War, between missile attacks and breaking news. Every guest came carrying a gas mask and a check. Days of insanity. Like most days here. Your Mémé said the wedding was a terrible mistake.

It took forever. Years. Your genesis became a never-ending work in progress. I woke up every morning, bitter. Hopeless. Looking in the mirror as I washed my face, I couldn't stop cursing myself. The world around me teemed and vibrated with violence. But I resisted, took a breath.

Then doctors. Tests and ovulation charts. Long nights of reluctant sex and sorrow. Two miscarriages, at ages twenty-three and twenty-four. Three weeks living apart. A cease-fire of sorts; she at her sister's, I mostly in the office. Back then, your mother and your aunt were still quite close. Can you believe that? Our apartment was a graveyard. I couldn't go near the place. It smelled of old Cheetos and mold. Black water kept dripping down the ceiling, the same problem we still have with the pipes. I made sure our bedroom lamp was on in case she wanted to return.

At long last, a reunion. Her favorite Italian place. I arrived twenty minutes early, hoping she would notice. She didn't. Lots of tears, half words. The only red wine on the menu that we could afford. A doggie bag. Later, pizza and red wine between the sheets—so unlike her—and lots of coffee in the morning, to take the nausea away. Life went back to normal, we believed. We decided to be patient.

One afternoon, a call. I was still an intern at Eisenberg and Co., still very young. Not quite a lawyer yet. But I was ambitious. Outside my window, it was raining like the End of Days. Your mother called me from a pay phone. It worked, my love. She sighed and said we made it. And with that sigh I became a father.

That *it* that worked was you, big boy. A few months later, you made your entrance. Like some biblical illumination. You were a perfect thing. Your father's nose, your mother's eyes. Your Mémé's long, slim fingers. You were as red as a tomato. Wrinkled, tiny. Lots of hair. Then the vessels of our life together broke, though not entirely. Your mother and I were left with shards. We did our best to cling to one another. The sex was good; you hate it when I say that, you think I overshare, although I simply speak my truth. But that bright Kabbalistic light was gone. Along came Tohu—an agent of chaos—seeping into our apartment.

You see, I've talked about this with Rabbi Ginsberg. More than once. These past few years, we've been in touch, Ginsberg and I. Today I know that you were the beginning of it all. My journey to enlightenment. You growing up, leaving my purview, *Blessed is He who has now freed me* and all that. Being your father has been the most terrifying honor of my life. When you were born, I was petrified. I felt deeply insufficient.

At first, your presence made me want to disappear somewhere, just like your mother's father, the skunk. But knowing I could not—would never—I wanted to have all the answers at the ready. Girl stuff, sure, that I could handle, but all sorts of other things as well, like decency and justice. And how to be a man.

He tells me things, the rabbi. He's a lovely person. I used to see him less, but now we talk several times a week, sometimes on the phone. Your mother, as you know, is not a fan. She calls him cynical and dangerous. A snake, a fox. Shylock from Jerusalem. Which coming from any other person in the world would be antisemitic. But coming from your mother, it's a simple observation. A scientific fact. I hope one day you learn that even when she seems extremely lucid, she's actually insane.

So here's what Ginsberg says, big boy. I've never told you this. My father, needless to say, explained none of it to me. The only religion he was willing to accept was hedonism, and only when it was his own. Your Mémé was a major victim of his selfishness, of course. These things that Ginsberg tells me, they're essential, ones you really need to know. Things that, even after years, your old man still tries to understand.

At the beginning, God was formless and adrift. Pure energy, that's all. He wanted to create something with a purpose and a shape. But then He realized that in order for creation to take place, He had to make some room for it—in other words, He needed to withdraw. So He pulled into Himself and decided to create a void, a space where He could make something out of nothing. Sounds crazy, right? I know. But it makes sense, yes, it's beautiful, if you actually listen with no cynicism and try to dig beneath the language of what your mother considers science fiction.

God made a hole. And from that hole, our entire world emerged.

My life together with your mother suddenly became a mess. The passion waned. It wasn't that there wasn't love. There was. Too much, I think. But suddenly there was this kind of overwhelming emptiness. Somehow, we couldn't get it right, the three of us—I, she, you always squeezed between us, sleepless, sweaty, in the middle of our bed.

I was absent. Wrapped up in my work and one-night stands. I was a kid, even though I looked like an adult, going to the office every morning with my leather briefcase. In a way, I think I still might be a kid. Funny, isn't it? Maybe it's because I never had my own bar mitzvah, since your Mémé was a Christian and my father was a scoundrel. A man-in-waiting, that's what I am.

I've made mistakes, big boy, most of which are still unknown to you. Ghastly ones. Immense. I've tried to climb the Tree of Life and fallen far too many times. Every fall has been horrific for everyone involved, including you. I've drunk myself out of two separate law firms. Spent nights with women whose names I can't remember. I've slept in parking lots and on empty streets, inside my car, on benches, covered in my piss. I've woken up in hospitals wearing nothing but my boxers. I told you that my motorbike had been stolen, but I sold it when I had to pay my debts. Your mother sighed and looked the other way until there was nowhere to look because we were surrounded by my sins. When they called her from the bank to ask about the money I had borrowed from your savings, she went ballistic. That was when she disinvited me from your bar mitzvah, Adam.

I want to be better. I think I can. I'm not quite sure I know what being better means. But I will learn. Besides, now I know what it doesn't mean. Which is not the worst way to begin, I guess.

I've spoken to Ginsberg about this at great length. He's a wise guy. Enlightened. He says that, despite all that has transpired—the lies and infidelities, the sacrilege, her fury, the loans and debts, your oddities—despite all that, there's hope. There always is for Jews. Your mother thinks that pretending nothing has been broken is the way to go; it's not. We should embrace the brokenness. In the Kabbalah, the broken vessels herald something good. New life. Redemption. It sounds so grand. But apparently, it's up to us, human beings, to bring that change about. To return the fallen spark back to its source, where it belongs, where it was first created.

Tikkun. Have you heard of that?

That's precisely why, big boy, I'm walking up the hills of Safed tonight, talking to myself. It's strange. My father told me once that walking makes your troubles fade. He wasn't wrong. I'm asking God to send my words to the illuminated hall where you now stand.

I try to picture what you may be doing now. Maybe something ordinary, like taking a piss or drinking orange juice. If

I were there, I'd let you try some Johnnie Walker when your mother wasn't looking. But who knows? Perhaps you're up to something more exciting. Your Mémé says that one day you'll surprise us all. Silent water runs deep, she insists. So maybe you're smoking your first cigarette. Hopefully not; I made that mistake when I was just about your age, and here we are. Maybe you're dancing with that girl you almost told me about when you missed the bus and had to take a ride with me. Your mother mentioned her at some point. I'm blanking on her name.

Is there someone in your life? I asked you in the car. What do you mean? you asked me back, and I said, Love. So you said, Oh. And then I asked again, Well, is there? You responded, No, and there was anger in your voice. So I said, Oh, okay. You took a moment to yourself, and then you asked me, Why? I smiled at you. I was just wondering. You said, Cool, and I asked, Will you tell me if there is? You said, What? And I said, Someone. You nodded, and I felt obliged to add, I don't care who it is. Then we both went silent. Is everything okay, Dad? you asked after a while. Nothing was okay; I was losing my grip on the world from day to day, but I said, Sure, why? And you murmured, I don't know. I smiled again. I'm just tired. Very tired. You? I asked. You didn't even take your time to think about it. You shrugged and muttered, Yeah, I'm good, I'm great. So I said, Great, and you said, You can drop me off right here. I kissed your forehead as I always do and then unlocked the door and let you leave. It wasn't until I lost your image in the rearview mirror that I wept.

Now it's late. The dark roads and the stone whisper something I still can't understand. Sometimes I think I'm a shadow. Those who notice me stop and tell me with their eyes that I'm crazy. But I'm focused on my mission. I barely even see them.

I have it all planned out. I even brought a map and rented a yellow Citroën from that car agency right by my office. I left my phone in the hotel where I've been staying. No distractions. I need to pay a visit to the rabbi. Not Ginsberg, this time. Isaac Luria. You may have read about him somewhere in your books, even though he might not be your cup of tea. He's quite well-known, I think. I am, of course, no expert. Some people call him the Ari. The Lion.

He died over four hundred years ago, but you could say that he is very much alive. I've always thought that we Jews have an odd relationship with death. We're very used to it, but we don't spend much time picturing what might be on its other side. It's such a shame. The rabbi rests not far from the old hospital in Safed. Right at the entrance to the cemetery, after ascending hundreds of stairs, Ginsberg said, I'll find a little cave. Inside it, I'll see a spring that gushes out of nowhere. This is where the rabbi used to bathe. The story goes that when he died, his pupils, who some called his cubs, brought his body there at his request. They let the water cover him, except his glorious head. Then his most beloved pupil knelt and whispered right into his ears, All that you asked for, Luria, we did. Now it is your turn. With that, the late rabbi opened his eyes, lowered his head, and completed the immersion of his body in the spring. When he was done, the pupils pulled him up, crying with disbelief, and buried him outside, next to the fence.

Today it's a mikvah where people go to purify their souls. Much deeper than it seems. The water is freezing, definitely now, but even in the middle of the summer. I've seen some pictures on the internet. It's natural, no fancy faucets, pipes, or marble floors or anything like that. Those who immerse themselves in it before they die make *teshuvah*; they repent.

The night is empty, and Safed is cold and wet, but I am no longer afraid. Now I know, big boy, I understand. We're all a little broken. You and I will learn to coexist. Somehow, sometime, I will make things right. I promise.

As I walk, I see the mountain that we climbed together years ago, where I resolved to shave your head like Ginsberg said, where you cried and cried and then went silent for what felt like an eternity. You probably don't even know what I'm referring to. Maybe one day you'll understand; being a parent is the most terrific pain.

I'm almost there. I can see the cemetery's gate. Thank God. Your old man is definitely out of shape. Remember how you and your mother used to visit me when I played basketball with my high school friends on Saturdays? I don't think you've ever been so proud of me. They demolished that court last year.

Oh, look—the gate is open. A cat just walked through, leaving it ajar. Maybe he, too, would like to bathe. Are cats capable of sin? Can they repent? I'll sneak into the cave where Ginsberg said I'd find a single bulb hanging from the ceiling, meant for *meshugges* like your father. I'll take my clothes off and breathe in the sweetness of the wind. Your name will be the only prayer on my lips, and I will whisper it into the void. And when I look down at the water, just before I dive, I'll smile, because I won't know if it's you I see in the reflection or myself.

Three Rings

1.

Hello?

Ben?

Yes?

We need you, Ben.

What?

We need you. You have to come back to the base.

When?

Now.

No. No way. I just got to the hall—

Ben. I'm sending Kaplan to pick you up.

Excuse me? Where?

To bring you here. He'll be there in an hour and a half.

You told me I could stay until tomorrow. I made plans, I can't just—

It's an emergency.

I can't. I'm sorry. You'll have to figure something out. I'm at my cousin's party.

It's starting, Ben.

What's starting?

Just be ready.

Can I go home first? Take a shower?

No. He'll text you when he's there. Be ready.

There is water on Mars, in abundance—most of it exists as ice—but it is yet to be seen whether it can harbor life. Mercury remains the least explored of the terrestrial planets. And Saturn has more than sixty-two known moons, although the exact amount is debatable because its rings are made of vast numbers of orbiting objects, constantly in motion. Even now, as Ben finishes the cigarette he rolled outside the banquet hall, rovers and probes roam in the deep, dark emptiness, new stars come into existence, entire planets perish.

In the meantime, Ben decays. Sooner or later the world will turn into a giant cigarette, just like the one between his lips. If we don't starve, we'll drown. If we don't drown, we'll go up in flames. Like in that poem that Ben's mother used to sing to him in elementary school. *You see, O earth, how very wasteful we have been.*

2.

Yaeli?

Yes?

Hi.

Hey, Ben.

How's it going?

Fine.

Where are you?

Home.

Are you mad?

Why would I be mad, Ben?

I don't know. I read your text again.

Which one?

You know.

The one I sent three weeks ago?

That last one, yes.

And?

Just wanted to check in.

Okay.

What have you been up to, Yaeli?

Is there anything you want to say?

I guess I want to hear your voice.

And?

What?

Ben.

What?

What do you want?

What do *you* want?

What do you mean?

You know.

I don't.

Okay.

What?

I miss you, Yaeli.

Fine.

Don't you miss me, too?

Ben. I'm tired. Please.

Do you miss me?

Ben, I—

Do you?

Yes. I do.

So?

I should go.

What?

Have a lovely evening.

Ben didn't think he'd make it here tonight. He hoped he wouldn't. The past few days have been a mess, just as he'd anticipated. A burgeoning catastrophe. There wasn't even time for him to grab a clean shirt from his closet at his mother's. He shut his eyes, and when he opened them, he was no longer at the barracks. His uniform still reeks of smoke. Every muscle in his body aches. He'd give his life for a quick shower. Although his filth is probably impossible to wash off. His whole existence: a massive wine stain on a napkin.

From outside, the hall looks like a spaceship. It vibrates in the darkness, glowing with kaleidoscopic mania. People rush inside, buzzing with excitement for the party. Ben doesn't think he knows them, which surprises him. Women in shawls and chiffon dresses, and kids running around like insects in a bottle. Men in jackets. Ben thought he'd recognize more faces. Watching the human swarm, he can see nothing but shadows, bodies.

Stop calling me, Ben.
Why?
Because you don't know what you want.
I want you, Yaeli.
You don't.
Okay.
I'm serious, Ben.
Fine. I won't call. Promise.
Thanks.
Will you come see me, Yaeli?
What? Where?
At the party.
What party? I thought you were at the border, in Nahal Oz.
They gave me an *after*.
I don't understand.
My cousin.
What about him?
His bar mitzvah.
Adam? Now? Are you there?
Yes. You can come here, too, you know.

Where?

To the party.

Okay.

Do you wanna? Come here?

I don't think so. Are you drunk?

I can pick you up. They said that Berta Schatz would be here, too, to sing.

What? Berta who?

It's hilarious.

Are you drunk, Ben?

Can I pick you up?

No, I don't think so.

I can take my dad's car, be there in, like, twenty.

I am busy.

Doing what?

Why did you call?

There are things I need to tell you.

Ben. You make me very sad.

I'm sorry.

Don't.

So?

Just stop calling me. Okay?

I can't. I need you. Please. Don't hang up, Yaeli.

Ben thought that maybe if he called Yaeli, she would tell him what to do or how to save himself. She's probably the only one he trusts. He wanted to come clean about his daily acts of self-erasure. And now he's pining for the feeling of his head against her breasts. Their months together seem like a hallucination. A dream that wasn't his.

He had to see his aunt Sarah inside, some of their family friends, his parents. And Adam, whom he hadn't spoken to in ages. *There's so much he can learn from you, Sarah* had told Ben last month at that horrendous Friday dinner. Ben knows there's absolutely nothing he can teach.

When he walked into the hall, his mother looked at him as if he were a ghost; he hadn't told her he was coming. He hadn't told her anything. As always, everybody had a question, and he had to tell them all the lies they had expected: a girlfriend, army friends, yes, he's still considering officers' course this coming spring. He has become an expert at this. A factory of half-truths, a one-man show. He wonders if it might finally rain tonight. He wants it to; he's always loved the winter. There are palpitating clumps of fury in Ben's chest. If he could smoke a joint, he would. But they sent his guy to jail. Six months. Possession and selling.

On the way from Nahal Oz, his unit's driver, Kaplan, told him he looked like a corpse. *Cheer up, my brother*—Kaplan slapped Ben's shoulder, which irritated him. *I feel as if I'm driving to a funeral, not a bar mitzvah,* Kaplan laughed. *Your eyes look dead.*

Ben wasn't dead. Not yet. He was shrouded in the foggy numbness of unfeeling. But Kaplan wasn't wrong; a sense of doom was growing in Ben's throat. The possibility of dying.

What, Ben?

What if I don't come back, Yaeli?

What do you mean?

From Gaza.

Don't—

Will you say that at my grave?

Listen. I really need to go. And you need to stop calling. Please.

Should I call your mother?

Yaeli?

Are you crying? Jeez—

Fuck you.

What?

I hope you get raped. Gang-raped. I hope you die alone.

Look after yourself, Ben.

I love you, Yaeli. Don't hang up. Please. Are you here?

Every now and then, Ben would wake up quivering, covered in sweat. His friends would be asleep. Those who'd still be up would be playing Snake on their phones or masturbating. He'd hear them toss and grunt. The hot creaking of their bunk beds. The room would stink of dirty socks, and he'd be cold under the thin wool blanket. Someone would fart and someone else would laugh. Ben would try to breathe. He'd shut his eyes and listen to the world. He'd hear the world succumb under its weight and crack, but it would never fall apart entirely. Now, as Ben finishes his cigarette outside the hall, he shuts his eyes as if he's still in bed and tries to listen once again. He hears it. *Crack*. Something just fell to pieces.

3.

The man talking on the phone in Arabic wears rings around three of his right-hand fingers. Ben finds that odd. Silver, silver, gold; index, middle, pinky. No wedding ring. Four silver bracelets. Ben thinks he's seen this man before but cannot place him.

The man is dressed in black. He's elegant. Tailored pants, a button-down with the sleeves rolled up, sleek shoes designed to look like leather. His many earrings sparkle even from a distance. He doesn't see Ben staring at him from the other end of the terrace, behind the banquet hall, that overlooks the beach.

Ben listens closely, trying to decode the stranger's words. He can glean only the few they made him learn in middle school and basic training. *Soldiers. Military car. Demolition order.* Words good for hardly anything but subjugation. The man is clearly in some kind of trouble. Ben smiles and wonders whether he should try to help him.

He wants to speak but doesn't know quite what to say and how. He'd have to raise his voice if he wants the man to hear him. He doesn't want to shout. Language is a problem. Hebrew makes some sense, but not entirely. English, in this context, just feels wrong. And Arabic he doesn't really speak. So Ben stays silent and preserves his smile.

The man hangs up and waves at him. Ben fumbles for words, then grasps the first that come to mind. Hebrew it is.

I'm sorry—
It's all right, soldier.

Want one?

What?

Do you want a cigarette?

Sure. Thanks.

Forget it.

They smoke. On the beach, children collect the final sea-shells of the day before their parents call them home. Someone on the winding road beneath the terrace honks. A drunk woman in a beautiful green dress laughs rau-cously. A beer bottle breaks and the glass shatters across the pavement. The woman wails and some dogs bark, responding from afar. Why did he have to be a dick? she yells. Ben thinks of Yaeli and of their last vacation at that bed-and-breakfast in Amuka when she said that she was leaving.

Now he remembers: yes, he saw this man inside the hall, carrying a drinks tray earlier. It was when Sarah was in the midst of her interrogation, questioning Ben behind the salad bar about his mother, Yaeli, Gaza, not even tak-ing in his terse replies. Sarah most likely didn't see this waiter. Ben did.

They clocked each other briefly. He thought the waiter looked at him like that because he didn't like the military uniform. Ben doesn't like it either; he has been fending off the urge to rip it off himself and burn it. But what if it was something else? Ben stares into the waves now, puckering his lips. The sun is gone. Clouds gather in the sky. Transformation, always, all around him.

So you're a waiter?

Yes, soldier.

How long have you been working here?

A couple months. To pay for my master's.

Your master's? In?

English literature.

Ooh la la.

That's French.

I see.

Nice party.

Is it?

One of the nicest I have been to here.

I think it's totally over-the-top.

Hataa al'ashjar tafahmuni.

What?

Nothing.

What did you say? I used to learn Arabic once, but—

Never mind. I'm sorry.

Tell me.

It's a poem.

That you wrote?

Frank O'Hara.

I don't know him.

That's a shame.

Yes? Is it?

He's my favorite. American.

I see.

I translate, sometimes.

Oh. I do, too.

You do? What do you translate, soldier?

People's faces. Or at least I try.

Oh. Okay. That one's tricky.

I'm not particularly good at it.

I see.

And you?

I translate poetry. Much easier, to be fair.

I'm not so sure.

Trust me.

Well, I guess you're an expert.

I'm really not.

What does it say? That poem?

I am the least difficult of men. Even trees understand me!
I'm just like a pile of leaves.

Funny.

Ben has never met someone who's handsome in this way; this guy's arched eyebrows, his stubble, the dimple on his chin. There is something remarkable about this man. It doesn't strike you on the spot but crawls into your consciousness, slowly making itself known, until you can't unsee it.

He feels an urgent need to learn the tiny details of this person's life, like how he drinks his coffee and whether he has

ever owned a cat. And even though he's terrified, he thinks
he wants this man to know him, too. He'd like to tell him
how colorless his life has been.

Ben knows the man is wary of his presence on this terrace.
He would be wary, too. And mad. Seeking silent privacy, this
guy would not have thought he'd come across a soldier here.
Ben tries to glimpse himself in the big eyes of this man. Up
close, he can finally identify their color: green. Are they a
window or a mirror? Neither. He expects to find exhaustion
or despair inside. But what he sees is horror.

Are you coming from the border, soldier?
Yes. And you? Where are you from?
The north.
Oh. Where, exactly?
Are you interrogating—
No. Hell no. It's just—
It doesn't matter.
Why?
You wouldn't know the place I'm from.
Try me.
Well, Yasif. Does that name ring a—
Yes, of course it does.
Liar.
I swear. I know Yasif.
What is it near?
Jaljulia? What? Wait, no, is it Taibeh?
Nowhere near.

The Triangle area, right? I'm pretty sure I've been—
I'm pretty sure you haven't.
So you are Arab?
Palestinian.
Right. And do you live there?
Where?
Yasif.
I don't. I left a while ago.
I see. Where do you live?
In Tel Aviv.
The city that never sleeps.
The city that always yells and cries. A baby-city.

He wonders if this person has considered outer space. Ben, of course, has been obsessed. Ever since he can remember, but especially in recent years. Every night, before he goes to bed, he spends at least ten minutes watching the live stream of the International Space Station on the official NASA website. Since the station orbits Earth once every ninety minutes, it experiences a sunrise or a sunset almost every hour. When that happens, the picture disappears.

But sometimes, if he's lucky, it remains. And when it does, it's really something. The closest you can get to god in 2009. A symphony of light and shapes and colors. He likes to tell himself that he is probably one of a few who actually watch it live. He doesn't know if that is true. He wants to think it is. From time to time, he can hear voices breaking through the silence. Conversations between mission control and crew.

Once, he heard someone—perhaps an astronaut—murmur, Fuck. Or maybe that was in a dream.

Ben would like more people to consider the prospect of leaving Earth and building something new. Now that everything is broken, what they need is a fresh start, elsewhere. Another opportunity. The first one didn't go too well. Will they ever manage to settle somewhere without colonizing, exploiting, ravaging? Maybe they could give it all another try. Maybe things would turn out differently.

That's funny. You're funny. What's your name?

Khalil.

Are you gonna ask for mine?

I'll just call you Joe.

Joe? Not Yossi?

I like Joe.

Yes. Like a cup of Joe.

Like Joe Goebbels. Or Joe Stalin.

I don't think they went by Joe.

Why are you here?

The bar mitzvah boy's my cousin.

I mean, why are you not with your friends down at the border?

My commander gave me an—

After?

How do you know?

I'm a prophet.

I see.

Right.

Right.

Thanks for the cigarette, Joe.

It comes with a price, Khalil.

A price?

I want a prophecy.

What do you mean?

You said you were a prophet.

Yes?

So prophesy.

I am confused.

What do you see?

Where?

In my face.

I don't see anything.

Go on, Mister Prophet.

What?

Translate. Please.

I see tremendous misery.

Where?

Between your eyebrows. You think you are the most broken thing this world has ever seen.

What else?

You crave a getaway. Something else. New life.

But?

But you are terrified. You're looking for an easy way out
of everything. Something quick and simple. *Clean.* You wish
you could be clean. You need to hate someone other than

yourself. You want to hate me. You think you should. It's easy. But you can't.

When Khalil kisses him, Ben wants to push him off and punch him in the face. But he stays still and cool. An iceberg. He holds his breath, aghast. And then he realizes that what he actually wants is to swallow this man, to whisper something brilliant and funny in his ear. Khalil's stubble tickles Ben. His hands are searching. His breath is sweet and warm; it smells of anise.

Then something old and deep inside Ben starts to melt. He wants to stop it, but he can't. He touches Khalil's face, which has gained a new fragility. He feels Khalil's nose, his lips. His soft, electric neck. He strokes Khalil's chest with his fingers, trying not to push too hard against his ribs.

He wonders if that's what leaving Earth first felt like. Gravity has lost its power. And now he's floating in the vastness, twisting in the air. An astronaut of sorts. He's never felt so light.

There are other lives somewhere. Yes. There are nooks of pleasure in this world. Ben can seek them, like a spaceman. They exist.

As Ben presses his tongue against Khalil's, he is reminded of a book he used to read obsessively in middle school, one that he hasn't read in years. It is the story of the *Pioneer 11*, the first space probe to encounter Saturn. Before the *Pioneer*, people used to think that Saturn had three rings at most. Today we know that there are many more, colossal, intertwined. Billions of chunks of ice, rock, and dust, at the very least.

By the time Ben was born, the world had already begun to end, but only few acknowledged it. At that point, the *Pioneer* had traveled to the farthest corners of the solar system. That was when people said it disappeared. But the *Pioneer* remained in space, obstinate, heading toward the center of the Milky Way and carrying a golden plaque: a message to the civilizations that it might encounter. No one on Earth could see it anymore. Its signal was too far, too dim.

Good Time

Yes, baby, oh, just take it in, right there, fuck, yes, it feels so good and I'm just, oh, I feel so, yes, when I first saw you with that, fuck, I mean just, oh, as you crossed the dance floor with your uniform and rifle, you made me literally sick to my stomach, you made me want to hide and throw up in some dark, distant corner of the hall, but now I feel just, fuck, I mean just, yes, it feels so good, myself inside your mouth, filling the deep red emptiness, feeling wet and firm and warm, and looking down at you, your eyes, my balls against your chin, stroking your face, I bet it is your first time with a man, not that you are bad at this, but, well, your tongue is shy, your hands create a mess, your lips don't know what to do against my body, I feel their hesitance, their hastiness, trying to decide whether to lick, to suck, to swallow, and now you grab my ass with your right hand, squeezing it as if it were a pillow, or an orange, why would you ever squeeze an orange, or my ass, god only knows, a cold, ripe Jaffa orange,

I've always hated those, always depended on the kindness of strangers, you know, always thought Blanche DuBois was a fantastic drag name, there must be thousands of them, Blanche DuBoises, all around this big wide world, they're onto something, yeah, and now I rub my hand against your forehead, sliding my fingers down your eyes, your cheekbones, cheeks, brushing them against your pulsing mouth, dipping my fingers in and moving them against your lips, your teeth, the soft warmth of your tongue, and then I hear you gag, yes, oh, right there, you moan almost inaudibly because I'm still inside your mouth, you brush your tongue against my cock, sucking down the shaft, covering my balls in your hot spit, oh, yes, so warm, just you and I, together on this terrace, one day I'll frame this night and hang it on a wall, perhaps at a museum if I'm lucky, some kind of Lichtenstein or Warhol, ridiculous, right, yes, and I wonder if maybe I should light another cigarette, I feel a painful urge from deep inside my throat, like the beginning of a scream, would that be rude, would it make you think I am uninterested, unkind, full of scorn and pity, which I am, and if I ever want to fuck you, will you let me, is this a one-time kind of thing, I have to say that even seeing you like this, kneeling in front of me tonight, taking me all in, makes me want to sing or light a firecracker like some people do on holidays and weddings, but this feels much more dangerous, it makes me want to fill the world with poetry, if you just raise your eyes and look at me right now, I swear I will just, yes, I will just, oh, and then I wonder if you felt that, too, when I was walking past you with that tray of cocktails, shots, and toasted chick-peas, did you know our bodies would be pressed against each other, sweating, steaming, they had no other choice, our bodies, they are much stronger than our will, and I just knew it, yes, your eyes were yearning for, well, like a cat, not love precisely, not even warmth, the eggshell of your brittle mas-culinity, your stubble, the three sad lines between your silly eyebrows, hardly visible in the extravaganza of this evening, strobe lights, red, blue, yellow on your face, your pumped-up chest beneath your olive shirt, you clearly like the gym, and just before you showed up on this terrace Ayad called and said he was concerned because the soldiers had come again and handed him a demolition order, I had no idea what to say or how to help, I just muttered, Let me call you back, poor guy, he and Mariam got married this past summer, I was there, and it was beautiful, I had a lot of hope for them, they haven't even finished building their front steps, he said they wanted kids, and now I reach to grab and squeeze your chest, wishing I could crush it, slapping it, rubbing your nipples that are suddenly so hard, pinching, my mama would be furi-ous if she knew about all this, I thought I saw yours, too, your mother, I believe, she's gorgeous, that silken hair, that neck-lace, and oh, those cheekbones, sharp, unmissable, like yours, she's dazzling, oh, yes, keep going, yes, you clasped her hands and kissed them like a knight, with tenderness, she cried a lot when she first saw you, you stroked her head and wiped her tears, my mama cries a lot as well, when she talks about my baba, when she says I have to take my stupid ass and get the fuck out of this country, not quite her wording, fuck, but baby, well, you know, she says my future is America, this place here is completely out of business, sooner or later it will all be gone, why spend your life begging for crumbs in Tel Aviv when you can eat the whole pie in New Jersey, she loves my poems even though she's never read them, I've never shown them to her, so it's not her fault, she gets the gist, trust her, she knows, she says I am her life, *hayati*, and her smile is radiant, yes, oh, baby, oh, keep going, yes, she is so proud of my accent whenever I speak English, probably because I never roll my *r*s, I say clearly, confidently, *rain* and *red* and *riveting*, Who did you get the accent from, my mother asks, Well, definitely not your father, and she laughs, he was a man of toil and silences, I want to say I got it from *The Simpsons*, but I say nothing, she sends me money every month in yellow envelopes, his compensation, he didn't die for naught, she has to say that to herself so she can go on living, oh, baby, oh, just lick it, there, I rarely visit, not that I'm ashamed, I mean, of who I am, or who I was, it's just that, fuck, now with my master's and my jobs, I haven't had much time, when I'm not teaching I am writing, when I'm not writing I am reading, when I'm not reading I am here at work, and honestly, I need a break from Yasif, I just can't stand the questions and the looks, the sea of kibbutzim and moshavim around, although I miss the olive groves, that bakery I used to love, it's gone, those bare white walls, the silence of the roads at night, but Mama wouldn't hear it, no, she'd rather die young there than live to a hundred anywhere else, not even with her sister in

Chicago, not that she is young, my mother, but she is beautiful, oh, trust me, baby, yes, even after all these years, she is as sharp as ever, they know, these women that we call our mothers, there is no hiding from them, no cutting corners, they have a direct line to our hearts, they read our sighs, our thoughts, the little twitches of our foreheads, they listen to the murmur of our souls, fuck, baby, yes, and now you press your face against my thighs, I actually don't remember the first time I had a penis in my mouth, strange, right, counterintuitive, you'd think the first time would be something that you can't forget, the emergence of a portal to a brave new world, a metamorphosis, but no, well, other times I do recall, oh, yes, that guy's apartment right off Shenkin Street, next to that small café, where he and I had cheap wine and sweet potato chips at three o'clock, or that one studio in Yafa with large, horrific paintings on the walls, and how sunrise came and the guy and I were standing naked on that balcony that overlooked the port where Jonah, who was swallowed by a fish, tried to flee his fate, god, what an imbecile, once even at a movie theater in Haifa, but that one doesn't count, that was a hand job, the guy was pretty old and pretty married, and he wasn't even pretty, not at all, I have definitely had sex at parties, several times, but never in my workplace, never with a *jundi*, soldiers have never really been an option on the menu of my sex life, not even as an appetizer, there is nothing appetizing about soldiers, not my cup of tea, they make me sick, so this is special, yes, I don't even know if you'll remember it, I know I will, I'll see you in my dreams, you will become a line break in my poems, I feel that you are different, that's what I'd like to tell myself, I know it by the way you asked me if I wanted one, yes, I do, I want one, please, a cigarette I mean, you didn't even say your name, I bet it's a cliché, what would Mahmoud Darwish have made of this, probably rolling over in his grave, poor fellow, although he also had his Rita, he prayed to the divinity in her honey-colored eyes, between him and the rifle, yeah, oh, yes, I once met a Jewish apostate who told me he'd been most sexually active in his years at the yeshiva, I wasn't sure if he said that just to shock me, I thought it was quite funny, though, the crossroads where desire and religion intersect, a lovely setting for an accident, fuck, baby, would you want to go together to the movies, I hear there is a screening at the Cinematheque, a Pasolini, I believe, it's fine if not, I know, you wouldn't want to be seen with me, I mean sucking me off on a backdoor terrace is one thing, of course, but watching a Pasolini, not to mention being watched by others, no, you're just like everyone, you think that I'm your id, your dabke-dancing liberator, yes, your channel to a wilder, freer self, no, you don't know me, fuck, why did you stop, are you not having a good time, babe, I hate this word, oh, baby, I can feel your breath now, sweet, I hear the music from inside, it's hideous, like always, and it is also true that we are not far from the beach, it's hard to see since it has gotten dark, but you can take my word for it, I go there almost every night after my shift, what story do the waves whisper tonight, you look at me, I pat your military head, you're almost bald, it's chilly, and now it starts to drizzle, Is everything okay, Well, you tell me, Sure, Cool, I'm close, you smile, and now there's patience in your movement, there's grace, you reach beneath my shirt and feel the hill that is my stomach, yes, you're right, I don't go to the gym, I'm not that kind of queer, you probably don't have a choice, do you, it tickles me, your hand, as I stretch my fingers and then close them in a fist until it hurts, screwing my nails into my flesh, oh, god, all I want is boundless love, this place is tearing up my guts, and is it raining now, oh, no, you didn't tell me anything about where you came from or where you might go after this, when you'll turn back again into the unspeakable thing I'm trying to forget you are, you left it to my wild imagination, which is very wild indeed, and even if I ask, you'll never tell me, but I won't ask you, no, no way, when Baba died, Mama insisted for at least two hours that he went to Nazareth, He'll be back, of course, don't worry, honey, I was a kid and even then I knew that wasn't true, the way her forehead shrank and wrinkled, I knew that she was lying, fuck, oh, yes, the next day we all went down to the cemetery, Mama and my sisters and the rest, the rest is silence, yes, the make-believe was over, baby, Baba died, word spread through Yasif like wildfire, no sense of privacy, they wanted to put him in the ground as quickly as they could, I hate to say this, but it felt as if I'd shed ten kilos in a heartbeat, after the funeral we all went to that big hall by the *masjid*, then back to our place, we put some chairs and teapots under the shade of the gigantic lemon tree that always seemed like it was falling, all I remember from that time is coffee and dates, and dates and coffee, women wailing, shouting, people stopping by and offering to cook or clean or take the trash out, even in the middle of the night, the head of the council came by, too, I knew he was quite ancient, but he was older than I'd thought, he told me I was a good boy, he didn't even know me, he said that I should be so proud of my baba, may god have mercy, I didn't understand, just smiled and muttered, Thanks, I don't think I understand it even now, is there a death less necessary and less glorious than that of the construction worker, and my father's life wasn't all that lovely, but I should still be proud of him, oh, yes, I know, a few months later we finally received compensation from the insurance company, Mama paid to build a new apartment for my sister Mira and her husband that she loathes, my sister Ibtisam finally got the nose job she'd been dreaming of, but Mama didn't know a thing, so beautifully naive, she would never have approved of that, of course, and I wrote poetry, some of which was bad, most was dreadful, one poem described death as a *yahudi* farmer on a tractor, others were just fears and yearnings, the attempts of my inchoate queerness to undo itself, to undo me, When will you finally start taking those ladies to the movies, they won't be young and beautiful forever, and nor will you, you know, Perhaps next week, or on the weekend after if I'm not too busy, Studying all day like that, what are you even trying to achieve, it is a lovely face you have, *habibi*, too bad you're a homo, what a shame, such waste, a few months after Baba died, I first read Maya Angelou, and that was quite the end of it, oh, yes, I mean just, fuck, do you like poetry at all, you don't seem literary I don't think, I guess, not quite your style, what do I even understand, you know what they say, don't judge a lover by his cover, and putting aside the crimes against my people, your cover's not too bad, you are a quick learner, I can tell, you're smart, you are amazingly unhappy, but you read the language of my body, and you hate your own, don't we all, ever heard of van Gennep's *Rites of Passage*, I read him once at university, back then I didn't understand, there is a threshold we must cross, you see, sometimes we have to leave everything behind and step out of who we think we are to really get to know ourselves, fuck, oh, right there, that's it, I'm very close, now just keep going, yes, fuck, oh, oh, baby, yes, I really needed this, but what is it, there, there . . .

behind the wall there is a face who is it looking a little pair of eyes a shadow or a spy or god no it's a kid a little boy with glasses staring gasping wait I blink and he is gone but it's too late now and I can't keep going when I see our terrible reflection in his face realizing what we've been doing then I swallow and I tell you stop I hear a wail is someone crying there no not a wail a speeding car no it's a siren from the bowels of the earth and people are running on the street and in the hall they're shouting and now there's blood I taste it in my mouth blood on my chest and on your face my hair my balls blood gushing from your ears blood down your eyes blood in the broken pipes behind us and the floor and on the concrete walls dripping from the sky not really blood but something else like rain it's thick we're soaked in it and then you roll your olive sleeve wiping your face asking me are you okay and I say yes but it is clear you don't believe me so I say we should probably find shelter right but then you shut your eyes and smile making your best effort to show me you're a man that you are not scared that you are happy that you did it that it really had meaning or maybe it was a transformation who knows you offer me another cigarette and I say are you crazy come on then I pull up my underwear and pants I breathe and suddenly it's cold and in my mind I see the boy's small glasses the siren still rings in my ears the rain and I say let's go in

III

INCORPORATION

The Day My Childhood Died

It is 1:20 in Yasif a Wednesday
and I am walking out of school
hopeful and clandestine, it's 1999
or 8, I am intoxicated by the air and I have
finally escaped the class of old *ustadh* Murkus
who teaches things I have no pressing need to know
and sneaking through the yellow gate I think
of how I asked him *Can I please relieve myself?*
politely just as Mama taught me and that wasn't
quite a lie but what I really wanted was to witness
once again the miracle of the illuminated hall
to glimpse the light that burned my eyes
the sight that took away my breath

and so I climb the road that has no name (like
all the other roads in our village) and I stroll
by Abu al-Walid's sweet corner thinking

maybe I should buy some halva for myself
something sugary to suck on as I walk
around then I remember that I have no money
since my sister Ibtisam bankrupted me last night
after we bet whether or not rhinos can fart and
anyway I don't have time today I'm busy walking
past Shawarma Johnny with its postapocalyptic smell
vegetable oil and cigarettes and chicken death and
petulant kibbutznikim who lunch delightfully
drinking their shawarmas down with Coke against
the backdrop of el-Asmar drugstore a ghastly land
of pills and bottles that I rarely visit, well, except
when Mama makes me every now and then
threatening that it will be my sole responsibility
if Baba ever has a heart attack

now the wristwatch that he gave me last week
for my birthday cries out that it's
1:28 so I dart across the street past
the supply store and the car dealer and the gas
station where I glance at Lady Rana's face
shining from a women's magazine she sheds
a tear and with her white teeth and her crown
she tells me all the way from Europe
(where she has naturally moved, the queen)
that beauty knows no nationalities and
I say *Lady Rana don't be mad I gotta run*
but I will catch you later as I turn

right by al-Balad Bakery where I used to snatch
leftovers with my friend Ayad before
he moved to Tura with his dad I wonder
if someone has even noticed that I'm still
in my imaginary bathroom as I think about
my tales of stomach bugs and diarrhea realizing
that I've finally left the village and the magic starts
to happen through the big side window where I stand

they are the world's most dazzling machine
with blazing eyes and elongated arms they bend
their knees and stretch and jump and swerve six
mighty spiders in leotards and tights they flood
the studio with their brilliance and spandex
grace and I am wholly hypnotized I finally
forget about the push-ups I have hoped to do but
never have and all the secrets of my dreams the poem
of the wingless bird and then the teacher yells in
a mélange of French and Russian that I can't quite
understand and I whisper to the ballerinas who
neither see nor hear me *You are fire* and my words then
form thin clouds of admiration on the window
the piano and the motion and the arches of their backs

and now I'm gliding down the highway clinging
to the guardrails every time I feel unstable no one
sees me and fortunately I see no one, well, except
for one old driver who picks his nose with great

determination as he waits for red to finally give way to
green *What will he find there, gold?* my baba says
inside my head but I don't laugh I let
my feet take me all the way down to the river
until the vastness of the wadi makes me gasp
where my sister Mira used to make love to her boyfriend
as Mama thought she was at evening class becoming
some kind of social worker when in fact
she was learning how to be a woman then
I find a friendly olive tree and lying
down I let my thoughts run free
as the piano rings inside my head I'm worn out
and terrified but somehow proud, then

Hey they cry *hey you there hey*
what's wrong with you you perv
and instantly they see me as an animal
Why were you looking at those girls you
stinky Arab so I start sprinting down the river but they
are after me their eyes are murder suddenly
I'm on the ground swimming with worms and leaves
they rip my wristwatch off my forearm they
examine the inscription saying *Birthday boy oh*
that is sweet you perv oh only twelve oh
mazeltov they cry and feed me heaps of mud
mazeltov you Arab fag you fuck they grab
my hair and pull it with their bicep strength

their sharp nails pierce my skull and
I'm so thirsty that my mouth begins to burn

and when I wake alone the riverbed is murky
my watch is gone and it is hard to see I give
my face a wash because I must and I decide
to go into the world and climb back to the highway
where I walk protected by the light of cars back
to Yasif my village where the streets are dead
the storefronts have been shut the air
is filled with strange new bitterness outside
our building someone burned a motorcycle and
the fire cries my name I close
the door behind me gently and when Mama yawns I smile
How was your day, habibi? from the darkness of her bed
the hot plates on the table fill the room with steam
so I can tell my sisters are not there and Baba's still
at the construction site he'll come home late
tonight I walk into her room but try to keep the light
off so we don't have to see each other just as
she wanted then I kiss her forehead slowly
wiping redness off my lips and whisper *Great*

Boys

He wasn't quite an ugly boy. Not at all. He always felt himself to be, but never was. He wasn't even ugly as a baby, which, to this day, he still considered an accomplishment. Occasionally, he was told he had a pleasant face, a long, smooth neck. There was nothing particularly unappealing about his average body, which he had hated ever since he could remember. But he was just never one of those people who, when you walk past them on the street—or, worse, when you eye them on the beach or in a club—inspire a strong urge to make them yours.

The bar, as Adam had expected, was tastefully unglamorous, reasonably busy, and comfortably warm. This was his first true visit to the city, at least the first he could remember. His first time in New York as what most people would consider an adult. He had come here as a baby with his parents for his uncle's wedding, which didn't really count. In the twenty years that had followed, the world had changed so much it was unrecognizable. His parents had gotten divorced, shortly followed by his uncle and his aunt, and several others in their family; Adam had reluctantly become a soldier; and the peace process, which had defined the era he'd been born into, had turned into a cruel joke.

Adam ordered gin and tonic. The room provided little hope and little comfort. The two-and-a-half-star review he'd seen online was accurate: *Underwhelming, but the drinks were pretty strong, especially by usual East Village standards.* Why did he want to disappear so badly? Perhaps it was the Spanish disco song that no one seemed to care for—not even the group of old gay men who, huddled and hunched over a table, seemed to be having a ball—or the pungent smell of patchouli aftershave. He tried to smile, though not too widely, and bob his head to the rhythm of the music, which was somewhat challenging to follow. No one looked in his direction.

He didn't like this strange invisibility, although he did appreciate the anonymity the city was so famous for supplying. Tel Aviv was full of people who had known him as a kid and still refused to see him otherwise. New York had seemed pristine, uncomplicated, at least when he'd been picturing it from his dark bedroom at his unit's base. Cleanliness, he'd come to learn, was not the city's strongest suit, and Carrie Bradshaw was nowhere to be found, despite his ardent hopes. Yet the two weeks he had spent in this unfamiliar place suggested that there was some truth to the cliché about not feeling lonely despite being alone.

The glitter-faced, redheaded bartender who consistently

tried to avoid his gaze made Adam want to scream and break his glass. He took another sip and checked his phone. Three voicemails from Mémé—the only person in his life who was still leaving them—which, for the time being, he decided to ignore.

Her Alzheimer's was getting worse, but she clung to life with her unrivaled force, consistently collapsing past into present. The current fog of her existence did not reduce her restlessness. Mémé had told him it was common knowledge that a soldier's salary was lower than minimum wage. She wasn't wrong. Would he be willing to consider staying with her best friend from her glory days as a flight attendant while in town? Adam thanked her, murmuring he'd have to think about it. He didn't want to burden anyone and hoped to find a room alone. But for Mémé, questions were merely a formality, so answers were irrelevant. "*Super*," she said and clapped. "She'll meet you at the airport."

The Mademoiselle, as Mémé called her friend, lived in a small apartment near Columbus Circle. She had starred in Mémé's fables ever since he could recall, alongside an ensemble of heroes and villains, many of whom were long-lost or dead. "She might even be—you know—a lesbian," Mémé had stage-whispered back in Tel Aviv, hoping that the detail would increase the asset's value on the homosexual market of his mind. "I think she used to have some silly boy toy when we worked together, someone she never really seemed to give a damn about. She has never gotten married, not even engaged, but I have never had the guts to ask. Who knows?"

The Mademoiselle's one-bedroom, rent-controlled apartment, for which Adam paid the reasonable price of nodding as she told tale after tale about the days of Mayor Koch, satisfied most of his needs. He settled into her dim living room, between tall piles of DVDs in English, Hebrew, Czech, and Russian and a heavily stained coffee table. Her lime-green velvet sofa, on which he spent his nights, grew on him as the days went by, although it never managed to accommodate his head and feet at the same time. The Mademoiselle insisted she had bought it from Meryl Streep's sister—"a lovely lady, absolutely stunning, it all runs in the family"—sometime in the eighties. As far as Adam and the internet were both concerned, Meryl only had two brothers. But that was a hill even a pedant like himself was not willing to die on. Every time the Mademoiselle referred to it as "Meryl's couch," he smiled and said, "Well, I am humbled." There were no pictures on the walls, which first surprised him, until the Mademoiselle explained she had to sell them recently. "This bastard city," she said, "will soon become unlivable." The only window in the room, which let in little light, overlooked the relics of a Hungarian bakery and an electronics store.

He quite liked the arrangement, which on a good day felt like something borrowed from an old French novel. Every morning, Adam woke up early and made coffee for them both in her half-broken all-American machine. He left the building long before his host even considered getting out of bed and returned shortly after she came back from her evening walk. She usually boasted of a bag of pumpernickel bagels she had bought on sale. Her job, if she even had one, remained a mystery to him. How did she support herself while living in Manhattan? Mémé, atypically, hadn't known the details. Every time he tried to broach the subject with the Mademoiselle, she flinched, or giggled, or recoiled. So, despite his curiosity—she could be a nuclear engineer, for all he knew—Adam politely let it go.

They shared a humble dinner, usually some kind of pseudo-healthy takeout. (She had been alternating different kinds of diets since her thirties, Mémé had explained, but nothing seemed to work.) Adam told the Mademoiselle about his day—a carefully redacted version, elaborating on the juicy details of the galleries and bookstores that he thought she'd like, almost all of which she claimed to know. He left out the descriptions of unsolicited dick pics on dating apps and guys who wouldn't return his smiles at subway stations. Despite what Mémé had suggested—her gaydar was notoriously broken—he couldn't place the Mademoiselle on the homophobic spectrum. Adam assumed she was at least an ally, maybe more, but sexuality was not something they spoke about, so he wasn't certain. She called him "sweetie," which he liked, and "handsome," which he found unbearable.

Sipping unsweetened coffee she reheated in the micro-wave, she said he ought to eat less sugar and drink more wine, to think much less and do much more. If only she could go back to his age; she spent most of her twenties worrying about the future and feeling generally miserable. Dreams, urges, and desires, she confessed, were never really in her lexicon, unlike his legendary grandma, who realized that every day was unrepeatable. Now it was too late for the Mademoiselle. She was living in a city that made her feel either too lazy or too old.

But she was glad to lead a simple life, as easy as it gets, at least until they kick her out of her beloved habitat uptown. Thank god she never listened to her mother, whom she exclusively referred to as "the Wicked Witch of the Midwest." No, the Mademoiselle did not become a single parent in her forties after all. If she had children, she wouldn't have the stamina to care, and would have nothing to bequeath them but her old subscription to the Met, due to expire in three months. Besides, she said, she loved living on her own, which Adam tried not to interpret as an intimation that his presence was unwanted. On most days, she didn't have much to report: troubles with the doorman, with whom she'd had a decades-long love-hate relationship; a controversial exhibition that made it to the front page of the *Times* (she apologized preemptively for butchering the artist's name); a slightly racist joke. After two weeks of such harmonious cohabitation, Adam wondered how often his host had actually crossed her threshold to the outside world.

His mother had insisted he should try to use his days abroad to get some rest at last, but Adam wasn't sure what doing that entailed. New York was bristling with art and possibility, yet never in his life had he felt less motivated, less ambitious. He thought this trip could help him kill off nasty habits, like avoiding mirrors, skipping breakfast, and watching porn with earbuds on his phone before falling asleep. At times, he considered going for a run in Central Park, which was so close to the apartment he could glimpse it through the bathroom window as he peed and brushed his teeth. Eventually, morning jogs remained a dream. He soon found that the city in November was too cold even for his Eastern European bones.

The setup was by no means perfect, but it was the closest Adam had ever gotten to the life he had envisioned for himself. He always wanted to become the wanderer he thought that he was meant to be and make a home in the cities of his dreams, which were perpetually bright and inexpensive and never hostile to the Jews. Next on his list: Paris (*À la recherche de* Gertrude Stein), then Vienna (Zweig! Mahler! Freud!). He wished to turn back time, to revert to his deracinated roots. To most people in his life this seemed ludicrous or vain. Adam didn't care. He knew that as soon as he regained his freedom in eleven months, he would have to pull off an escape plan. The song of the diaspora was playing in his ears, making him wonder if one day, he might learn to dance to its reviled rhythm. Those who stay are likely to become impervious to hope, he thought. Hard places make one hard. But leaving seemed impossible. It was a privilege and a renunciation. An admission of defeat, so unlike him. This visit, in ways he still couldn't articulate, had made him hopeful.

Perhaps it was the great-uncle he had met for lunch at a vegetarian eatery in Chelsea that used to be a sleazy club—his only openly gay relative—who'd told him that the city had the magic power to erase histories, forge new identities, and alter fates. "I came here in the seventies, afraid even of the shadow of my faggotry," the uncle said, ingesting a spoonful of roasted Brussels sprouts. He didn't look at Adam; he fixed his eyes on the small cracks in the wooden table as he lectured. "Did I lose too many friends and lovers to that damned disease? Of course. Did my father keep insisting I was dead to him until his last breath? Sure. And still, my life is not the tragedy they always told me I was destined for."

Now, staring at the bartender again—to no avail—Adam knew his uncle could be right. The city made his misery a little sweeter. He finished his first drink and ordered another one immediately. Adam had chosen this specific dive bar for a reason. So far, his fortnight in New York had been embarrassingly sexless. Pictures of faceless genitalia never turned him on, neither the gaping anuses nor the mighty cocks. No. Adam was a sucker for the real stuff—voices, eyes, lips, moles on necks, a nice cologne.

However, this time, he wasn't on the lookout for a hookup (which, if the past was to be trusted, was likely to leave his meager self-respect diminished anyway). There was one last thing he had to do before he left. This was his final opportunity. He thought he'd gotten all the details right, but now he wasn't sure.

The playlist entered ABBA territory, which Adam thought was a prerequisite for all gay bars. So far, he didn't love the way the evening was unfolding. He wondered if he'd already become a creep, something Abbie had warned him of at least ten times before he left. She told him he should never look at anyone for more than fifteen seconds, especially if they avoid reciprocating. These days, she said, staring was a form of violence. "Despite what Hitchcock's sickening male gaze makes us think, voyeurs are never sexy in real life," Abbie explained. He trusted her, as usual, although Hitchcock was one of his all-time idols.

Some of the boys around him at the bar made him want to look at them for days on end. Adam had already learned with a considerable amount of pain that he possessed a tendency to conflate beauty and truth. He hoped that could be fixed, but feared it couldn't. Feeling the coldness of the second drink against his hand, Adam imagined himself dying alone in a minimalist, overpriced Chelsea loft.

Across the room, he recognized a semi-famous actor from a television show he used to watch with Abbie. He felt an urge to text her, but immediately remembered that his evening was her morning; she would be far too busy to respond. The actor's abs threatened to break through his red spandex shirt. His wolfish teeth were whiter than a newly painted wall. Despite the clear deception of the actor's body, thoughtfully devised to appeal to boys like Adam, he couldn't help but feel attracted—which, given the futility of the attraction, made his night feel even more dismaying. Only then did Adam realize that there was not a single woman at the bar. Halfway between the actor and himself, he clocked the person he was looking for.

A few days earlier, Adam had been shocked to stumble

on a picture of this man in an obscure literary magazine at a café in Williamsburg. He had to take his glasses off and view the picture up close. He thought he recognized the face but wasn't positive. Adam Googled the name, Khalil Barakeh, and started going through the search results, which left no room for doubt. It was the waiter he had seen at his bar mitzvah with his cousin Ben. What was he doing in America?

Adam spent at least an hour reading Khalil's poetry and essays. In all of them, Khalil identified as a Palestinian in exile, but Adam couldn't find where he'd been born and raised. While many of the poems were available for free online, some were protected by a paywall. Adam was so enthralled that he subscribed to three magazines whose names he'd never seen. The texts were beautiful. The details all made sense, but he just had to find out more.

For a while, Adam was stymied. He tried to wipe Khalil's name from his memory, but it persisted, like an alarm that he could snooze but not turn off. It wasn't fate; it was an opportunity, and Adam would be crazy if he let it slip away. How often does the past come knocking on your door? He had to find where Khalil was. Besides, Adam was already complicit, like it or not. He'd let himself become a cog in the machine of domination. What's another act of espionage?

Eventually, Adam succumbed. He sent Khalil's name to Yogev, his only quasi-friend from his unit, and emphasized that any information would be useful. Yogev said it sounded iffy; the last thing he needed was getting into trouble four months before his long-anticipated discharge. But Adam made an offer Yogev wasn't able to refuse: covering guard duty for three weeks. Khalil wasn't in the system. His last name was extremely common. Yogev found thousands of potential relatives, from Jalamah to Yatta, even in Gaza. Maybe Khalil had changed his name, or simply wasn't from the Territories, in which case he was most likely a citizen of Israel and wouldn't have a file. Either way, Adam's investigation hit a wall.

But he couldn't just throw in the towel. He turned back to his independent research. Pictures, interviews, videos, reviews. It was an obsession, and even knowing there was something wrong about it, Adam couldn't stop. In one article, Khalil was asked to respond to the Proust Questionnaire, which uninspired journalists admired. His "idea of happiness" was spending a night at his neighborhood bar on Sixth Street, between Avenues A and B. Khalil admitted that it sounded lame but promised that it was, in fact, spectacular. Feeling a strange sense of accomplishment, Adam found the bar's address online and saved it on his phone.

Now the bearded, long-haired man from the picture in the magazine was staring into space, only a few meters away from Adam. A younger, prettier Walt Whitman. Adam recognized his eyes, even behind the thick-framed glasses.

"Is everything okay?" Khalil asked him, suspicious.

Adam cleared his throat. What could he say to start a conversation? "I think I know you."

"I beg your pardon?"

"I'm sorry." Adam cleared his throat again. "I think we've

met." He grabbed his phone and moved closer to Khalil, not knowing where he found the courage or how he might explain what he'd just said.

Khalil grinned. "Oh, are you Jeremiah's friend?" he asked. "If so, please tell him he can go to hell."

"Um, no—"

"Where do you think you've met me, then?"

"I guess—"

"Did I fuck you and never call you back?"

"No," Adam muttered. "That's not it."

The man paused. "Well, I don't think I've ever seen you, honey," he said. "And if I have, I do apologize. I'm sure you're fabulously unforgettable. My memory just tends to be on the defective side these days. So you should take everything I say with a little grain of salt."

His accent was so slight it almost went unnoticed. But the brief hesitance before each *r*, which Adam was familiar with, gave him away; he wasn't *from* New York. Adam had read somewhere that it was rude to ask questions about one's ethnic background in America. He didn't want to overstretch his chutzpah muscles, which he'd always deemed too weak at any rate. Besides, he didn't know what he could say without sounding deranged. So, still not drunk enough to be direct, he smiled and swallowed.

"What's your name?" Adam asked.

"Khalil," he said, taking a sip. "And you?"

"I'm Adam."

"Nice to meet you."

On any other night, Khalil would probably have faked interest in this youngster's life. At the very least, he would have asked him to say something else about himself, even just out of the American politeness Khalil had perfected. But tonight, Khalil was far too beat to make the effort. There were papers to be graded, texts and emails to be read and written, long-overdue bills to be paid. His vision for the evening had been simple: some whiskeys, awful music, then home—six blocks away—most likely on his own.

The silence gradually became oppressive. Khalil looked around, drinking his Glenfiddich in small sips and drawing long lines with his finger on his cheeks. Adam stood up, stretched, and left to use the restroom. Only when the counter started to vibrate did Khalil realize the boy was gone.

At first, Khalil assumed that the vibration was a daydream. He'd gotten used to the occasional hallucination. The other day, as he was crossing Washington Square Park after a seminar, he saw his father smoking a hookah with a gang of sleek-faced teenagers. It didn't bother Khalil that the old man always hated hookahs, not to mention had been dead for thirteen years. Khalil was a poet (hyphen anthropologist slash activist), at least as far as his self-made Wikipedia entry was concerned. Fantasies were something he should thrive on.

Within seconds, he identified the predictable source of the mystery: a phone. Adam must have left it there. Who does that in New York? Khalil was curious, but didn't have the energy to pry. Then something caught his eye, holding his gaze in a manner both irritating and irresistible. On the screen, he recognized a word.

Ima. Mother.

It was the first word Khalil had muttered as a baby, which had made his mama more concerned than proud. He mumbled it again now, trying to swallow down the bitterness it left inside his mouth. That aftertaste was Hebrew, a language he had barely spoken in eight years. He still thought sometimes about his hellish flight from Ben Gurion to JFK. His tears upon takeoff, as he saw the coast slowly turn into a faded line, dotted with the mosques of Yafa, then disappear. His silent promise to himself that he would scrape that language off his mind, no matter what it took. When the flight attendant smiled at him and asked in Hebrew, "Beef or chicken?" Khalil had resolved to answer a perplexed "Excuse me?" in the best American accent he could muster at that point.

The boy was back, looking lost and tired. He seemed like a completely different person. He was by no means more attractive. If he was interesting or kind or bright, Khalil couldn't see it. But suddenly there was a mystery to him that Khalil had to solve.

"So, where are you from?" Khalil asked.

Wiping his wet hands on his jeans, Adam was visibly surprised; he thought their chat had run its course. "I'm from Tel Aviv," he said. "And you?"

"I live around the block, on Bowery."

Khalil realized that his words, not quite an answer to the

question he'd been asked, could create the false impression that he had an interest in the Israeli. But he didn't care. His mind was busy trying to gauge Adam's age; clearly not a child, not even a teenager, but not quite an adult.

"I know you all have to serve in the military, right?" Khalil asked.

"We do," Adam said.

"Did you? Serve, I mean?"

"I did. Still do."

There used to be a time when Khalil could maintain clearcut dichotomies between innocent civilians and harrowing colonialists, carriers of olive branches and carriers of M16s. Then there were gradations, levels of differentiation. There were *yes buts*, *wells*, and *it's complicateds*. Ways of trying to make sense of the absurdity of what he used to call, in his naivete, the Situation. Not anymore.

"Where do you serve?" Khalil asked, attempting to disguise his curiosity by staring deep into his glass.

"You wouldn't know it." Adam hoped that he could dodge the question, but the impatience in Khalil's widening eyes made it clear he couldn't.

"Try me," Khalil said.

"The Civil Administration?"

"Of course."

Khalil knew exactly what this meant. Adam was serving in the West Bank, which was a different order of offense. Khalil's familiarity with the Civil Administration was deeper than he would have wished. It was the long arm of that amorphous entity that had signed the demolition order on the house where his friend Ayad lived with his wife, Mariam, in Tura; that had permitted his great-aunt to get her heart surgery in Haifa. The Civil Administration that was anything but civil. Two magic words that, in their brutal, bureaucratic omnipotence, could save a life just as easily as ruin one.

"Why did you come here, Sgt. Pepper?" Khalil asked.

"I had to take a break," Adam explained. This wasn't quite a lie; it was reality, abridged and bowdlerized—his favorite edition.

"So you just got on the first plane to New York?"

"I'm on vacation," Adam said, then added, for a reason that he couldn't understand, "Someone broke my heart."

This version was much closer to the truth, but not in its entirety. Adam had preferred to leave some major parts untold. His mother was getting lonelier, refusing to admit that she was struggling, which only made her struggle worse. His father was still licking the wounds after hospitalization in a psychiatric ward. They hadn't spoken in six weeks. Yishai had vowed never to return to that accursed institution, not even for a checkup, which Adam found reckless and understandable. Last time Adam asked, Mémé told him that his father had moved into a new house in the Negev with his girlfriend, Shelly, and her kids. Adam had promised he would visit once he got an *after*, knowing that he wouldn't. His hours at the administration felt longer every day. Abbie was far up north, living on some base near the Sea of Galilee and tutoring lone soldiers. According to her stories, the soldiers were more interested in her decision to avoid shaving her armpits, whose hair peeked sometimes through her green fatigues, than the rules of Hebrew conjugation that she taught.

Adam tried to make new friends as she encouraged him to do but felt that he could no longer sustain a conversation with folks who weren't Abbie. He never knew quite what to ask or where to put his hands. Every interaction with the people in his office pushed him closer to the edge of hopelessness. As a teenager, he had been anxious at the prospect of mandatory military service for reasons like having to share a shower every day with naked men. This turned out to be the easy part.

On paper, Adam was a noncommissioned officer, working at what the military called a DCO, a district coordination office. They made it sound as innocent as possible; the army, they insisted, had to remain immune to politics. He spent most of his days reviewing documents and issuing certificates, governing the lives of strangers through a regime of convoluted permits—to build, to study, to cultivate their land, to work.

Two years ago, during the first few months of training, Adam still had faith in the importance of his job. The sorting officer had said they'd teach him Arabic—the spoken language, not the Modern Standard version that he had to learn in middle school. They'd educate him on the Palestinian Authority, its apparatuses and inner workings. This seemed like something Adam could—should—do. Their mission, his commander told him, was to improve conditions for the local population.

Adam had had some aspiration of changing the system from within, but quickly learned that it was programmed to perpetuate itself. As time went by, he could no longer pretend the whole thing didn't make him sick. He couldn't eat. He couldn't sleep. Back home, life worked in binaries: here-there, us-them, peace-war. At the Jenin DCO, where Adam was eventually stationed, everything was muddled. Every day felt wrong. Having so much power over people while telling himself that he was still someone who wanted to do good became untenable. In high school, Adam had majored in psychology, a subject that he now dismissed as too abstract. But every now and then, he found the knowledge useful. Even though it was by far the lowest grade on his diploma, Adam could diagnose himself with cognitive dissonance, a condition that he shared with everyone he knew.

"I guess I need to stop falling in love with narcissists," Adam said.

"Oh, honey . . ." Khalil sighed. "Don't we all?"

Khalil examined Adam for the first time, head to toe. He realized that even if he tried, he couldn't hate this boy, his deeply bitten nails, the tremble of his voice. This Civil Administrator held so much contempt for himself that there was no room for others to pile on.

"What are you drinking?" Khalil asked. "This one's on me."

A few minutes later, they clinked two glasses of Negroni, each adorned with an ice cube and an orange slice. "*L'chaim*," Khalil said with a crisp *ch*. "I hear that there is not a single gay bar left in Tel Aviv, the queerest of all meccas. What happened? Have the Chosen People finally transcended the boundaries of sexual orientation?"

"This is my first time at a gay bar," Adam lied, "so I wouldn't know."

"Well, here's to many more."

The truth was that Adam had spent almost every evening in New York in a setting that looked not unlike the present one. He'd even come to this bar two days earlier to try to find Khalil. The exceptions were the day he landed, when his jet lag got the best of him, as Abbie had predicted; the night he went to *Sunset Boulevard* and spent two hours waiting for an autograph from Glenn Close, who had prior engagements, according to the bouncer; and the evening when the falafel at that Israeli food cart, of which he'd been suspicious, gave him food poisoning—a sign that he was truly in New York.

What had he hoped to find in those dimly lit, poorly ventilated, overcrowded caves that didn't feel like halls of self-empowerment, whatever that word meant? Where had his freedom-fighting heroes from the previous century—trans warriors, queer shape-shifters, faggot martyrs—all gone? Perhaps the carnival had moved elsewhere and he had missed the memo. Sitting on the pleather swivel stools, alternating cocktails with ginger beers, and eating through his humble budget, Adam had not experienced a hot rush of camaraderie. His nights out felt less like dancing at the party he'd been yearning to attend since his first erection and a whole lot more like eating cold, hard-boiled eggs at the shiva of a distant aunt he'd never known.

"Have you ever been to Tel Aviv?" Adam asked Khalil, although he knew the answer.

"I have not," Khalil lied. "I'm afraid I can't afford it."

"You should go."

"I might. If I can find the means and time, I will."

The bartender changed the music after repeated pleas from two guys who explained that if he played more Swedish pop, they might throw up. Now, for the second time this evening, Bonnie Tyler was holding out for a hero.

"What do you do? In life?" Adam said and quickly added, "If I may ask."

"Oh, sure. I teach. Anthropology, literature. And I write, too," Khalil said. "Some academic stuff. But mostly poems."

"Can I hear one?"

Khalil's impulse was to refuse—this was neither the time nor the place to share his work—but he considered the request. He hadn't written anything in months. He tried to think which of his old verses he could pick. Perhaps the one about the mornings when he was so petrified he couldn't crawl out of bed even to make himself a cup of tea? Or the one about how he had fled the only place he loved, the way his ancestors had done, because the savagery in Gaza had crushed his soul?

"Sorry," he said, defeated. "It's probably too late for a poem."

They remained silent for a while, each steeped in his anxieties. Adam recalled the last—and first, and only—time he'd seen Khalil: the night of his bar mitzvah, after his mother gave her catastrophic spiel. After he slipped away, in dire need of solitude and air. Before the siren, which he'd thought, at first, was the intro to a song. A backdoor terrace, illuminated only by the lights of passing cars. His cousin and Khalil, sharing a moment of ecstasy of which he was the only witness.

Then, later, in the ladies' room, where Adam had locked himself in panic, alone, devising his escape. Just before Abbie showed up and suggested that they change clothes; he squeezed into her dress, she put on his suit. In a building filled with family and friends, he could only think of Khalil. It was this man, that moment, that thrust Adam into the future, that made him feel less lonely in this world, less of an aberration. He looked for Khalil in the hall after the siren; he even checked the kitchen and the office. The man was gone. Adam remembered having tried to make sense of his overwhelming need to talk to Khalil. How could he miss someone he didn't even know?

Now, through the thick lenses of Khalil's glasses, he saw his own face doubled and distorted. What could he say? Every sentence he considered seemed too awkward. Should he explain? Apologize? Express his guilt, regret, fear, gratitude? He wasn't even sure if that was what he felt. His psyche had become disorderly, unreachable. Sometimes he wondered if he could ever find a way to undo shame, the organizing principle of his existence. There used to be a time when he was able to enjoy the company of his own thoughts. He was too young to hate himself like this. Or maybe he was too old not to?

What might happen if he told Khalil that Ben was now a

husband and a father, holed up in a cottage with a wife somewhere in the bedlam of Jerusalem suburbia? Khalil would laugh, if he even remembered who Ben was. Ben had been prematurely discharged from the army on what they labeled "mental grounds." These days, Adam saw his cousin once or twice a year, when people on his mother's side married or passed away. He didn't spend much time thinking about Ben otherwise. When he did, the thought was usually accompanied by some amount of indignation. To him, the lies his cousin lived were, more than anything, a crime against himself. Tonight, in what started to seem to Adam like another universe, he pictured Ben—stolid, silent, strong, incredibly repressed—and mostly felt compassion.

Then Adam thought he saw a glint of recognition—brief, almost imperceptible, but real—in Khalil's face. Just as Adam was about to ask about that day, years earlier, when they first crossed paths, Khalil stood up, grabbed his jacket, and said, "Let's go for a walk."

❧

They strolled in silence, without a clear plan or direction. They passed liquor stores and laundromats and bars and delis, walking at a steady pace and looking only forward. People were still out and about—drinking, laughing, chattering— but no one took note of the unlikely pair. It wasn't quite as cold as Adam had expected, so he forgave himself for having left his jacket at the Mademoiselle's. Khalil had hoped to take him to the river, but finally they reached a fence that hadn't been in place two weeks before.

For a change, it wasn't sex or even validation Adam was after. What did he want from this man, essentially a stranger? He didn't know. Mémé often said humans were creatures of connection, that paths crossed and diverged and, if they ever crossed again, it was always for a reason. He wanted to believe her. But traversing the East Village with Khalil tonight was crippling. Adam asked himself how people measured and defined their distance from each other. Khalil felt closer than anyone Adam had met since he had landed in the city. Perhaps there was no way or need to measure.

"The truth is," Adam said at last, responding to a question that had not been posed, "whether or not you're willing to admit it, you're basically alone. Even when you tell yourself that you're with others."

Khalil smiled. "Did you ever think that it was going to be different?" he asked.

"I thought it would get easier, at least," Adam said. "Well, not immediately and not entirely, but gradually, as time goes by. I used to think something would happen, that there would be a point when I'd feel good—not even good, just fine—about it all." He swallowed. "Does it ever get, like, easier?"

"What do you mean?"

"I don't know. I probably sound stoned. Or stupid. Never mind, forget it."

"No. You don't."

Adam was silent. "I guess I mean being a person," he said. "Being yourself, whatever that entails. Maybe it gets clearer, or easier, as you grow somehow?"

Behind them, cars swooshed down the avenue. An airplane started its descent. Khalil wanted to say the soothing words Adam had hoped to hear, to wrap the dullness of his life with colored paper and hand it over like a present. But he just muttered, "No."

Adam's flight to Tel Aviv would take off in seven hours. He would have to finish packing in a hurry and leave the lilacs for the Mademoiselle in the small vase by the door. This time tomorrow, give or take, the ordinary rhythm of his life would resume. He sighed, stroking the fence with his long fingers. He couldn't stand the thought.

What if he stayed just for a few more days? What if they removed their clothes and jumped into the dark gray stream? Like two boys on vacation, in their underwear, they could pretend it was the Middle Eastern summer they both loved and hated. They would wipe sweet watermelon juice from their lips that would stick to their hands and stain their chests with thick red splotches. And they would burst out laughing at a joke only the two of them could understand, then climb and jump over the fence. They would hear the faint cries of their mothers—*Dinner! Dinner!*—like distant wind chimes, reminding them that they are loved somewhere. The water wouldn't be as freezing or polluted as it seemed; it would gush, buzz, glitter, make their necks and shoulders glow. Their bellies would peek above the surface of the river, like little buoys, smeared with moonlight. And in their make-believe, just for a moment, life would be open, not like a wound but like a door.

Adam rested his face against the fence, feeling its silver coldness with his forehead. The river flowed, contaminated, unperturbed. "It's late," he mumbled, and already regretted what he was about to say. "I gotta go back home."

The Curtain

You're standing silently behind the curtain, savoring the privilege of seeing without being seen. Your best friend's dress is shimmering with turquoise sequins. It feels too tight against the sharpness of your ribs. Your belly's bulging out, reminding you, again, that you are thicker than you'd like to be. You smile at no one in particular. The makeup she applied so carefully to your face back in the ladies' room—concealer, lipstick, blusher, a powder of some sort—turns you into something of a clown. You've always hated clowns; you find them hideous, even at thirteen.

Tonight was meant to be your party, but the world had other plans. You shut your eyes, rub your wrists and elbows, try to breathe. It is a spectacle, you tell yourself in an attempt to slow your pulse. None of this is real.

Behind the curtain, in the hall, there are too many shadows. Dark, slowly moving shapes that have no names. They are more graceful than forbidding, like the dancers you adored at the ballet or the surrealist paintings at your grandmother's favorite gallery in Rome. You try to guess which shadow is your mother's. You know she's there, but it's impossible to see.

You hear voices, none of which you recognize. The siren that went off earlier still rings in your ears. Throughout the country, people will talk about the tanks crossing the border. Ministers will migrate to television studios, singing hymns of sovereignty and pride. The world will shrug and carry on. Everyone you know will speak of might and blood and fear.

Someone in the hall—you don't know who—insists on the importance of combining ground warfare with air strikes all at once. Someone else says he hasn't been able to get hold of his kids.

You try to focus on the other voices, pushing the ones that make you anxious to the margins of your mind. The moving chairs. The broken plates and glasses. The soft hum of the stage. The slow death of the party. The rain outside, still drumming on the hall's thin ceiling. The throat-clearing. The sighs and the farewells. The exchanges on the phone. Relief and shock. *Where are you? Can you hear me?*

Even though you wouldn't look at your reflection in the mirror, you know the dress looks great on you, much better than the silver suit you hate. Wearing that suit, which she convinced you to take off, your best friend looks like a gangster, but not a scary one. She is staggering.

You make a list of all the people in your world, the many characters in what you used to think of as a one-man show. You see them right in front of you, as if projected on a screen.

The night you tried to bake banana bread with your best friend and almost burned down her mother's kitchen. An elevator with your parents, on the way to what was probably their last Seder together; that time you saw them kiss. Your past, illuminated on the curtain. And behind it, in the hall, your future—a mystery, but not a horror film.

Something is happening behind the curtain. You shut your eyes. You can hear music from afar, getting closer, like the circus that came to Tel Aviv when you were very young. Now you see them in the hall. First, the waiter from the terrace in a red velvet tailcoat and a black top hat, clasping a baton, proud, energized, a sublime master of ceremonies. Here's your mother, her face powdered, blowing into a cornet, cheeks puffing. Behind her, your best friend, carrying a tuba bigger than her head, dressed in a sequined jumpsuit and a floral jacket. And look, here's your grandmother, red-nosed and rosy-cheeked, in a Jazz Age golden robe, playing a pink French horn. And your cousin. What is he holding there, a rifle? No. A clarinet. He's wearing a red polka-dot dress, a cloth strip tied around his waist, and a tiny hat on top of his tricolored wig. After him, your father in a ball gown, with the mustache that he used to have when he'd just met your mother, beating a tin drum harnessed to his neck and smiling. Lagging behind but not too far, the DJ, with a neck ruff, a bulky blouse, and pantaloons, all white, clutching a triangle, which he strikes on cue from the waiter with a tiny metal stick. They march together, left, right, left, crossing the hall in perfect synchrony.

All the guests are there, even the ones you haven't met,

ecstatic. They form a circle in the middle of the room, clasp hands, and dance, dance, as if they've lost control of their limbs. Is it a hora? Dabke? They don't seem to know or care. Every now and then, when they can no longer contain their joy, they cry out, *Hey! Ho!* The band plays on. Your heart expands. You want to join them, to take part in their merriment. Not yet. You will.

Open your eyes now. Swallow. You're alone. The singer who promised she'd perform with you tonight will probably not be here. Another war is in the making. You'll never see your parents kiss again; tonight they stop being your parents and start turning into something different, new. The structures of your life, the ones that you believed were keeping you afloat, have spectacularly crumbled. But beneath them you'll find a shining thing. What will it be?

No, the singer will not come. You'll have to fill her shoes and sing onstage, wearing your best friend's dress, alone. Violence will rage again, and days of hopelessness will follow. You'll soon discover that the world is much more broken than you think.

No one knows you're there, behind the curtain. Except for your best friend, of course, who's standing where the DJ sat before he disappeared. You'll see her on the other side. She knows it all; she's known for years. For the others, you have been a ghost. You realize that once you cross the threshold, things will change. The day, strange and electric, feels like an adventure that is yours entirely.

Yes, things will change; they always do. You rarely notice it because the world is fast. But now you see. It won't be instantaneous or swift or anything like what you had in mind. It won't be clean. It might take years, a lifetime. When did you stop being a kid?

You will be brave. You will be fine.

Breathe.

Mazeltov. The wait is over. Your new life finally begins.

Acknowledgments

Having moved into literature from the more explicitly collaborative arts of film and theater, I'm often baffled by the notion of the writer as a solo player. This is an idea that *Mazeltov* wishes to challenge. No artist is an island. Even though the number of people who have midwifed this novel into being is far too great to count, I'd like to extend my heartfelt gratitude to:

My editor, Riva Hocherman, whose brilliance, passion, and integrity have made this a transformative project and me a better writer. I'd like to thank the glorious team at Henry Holt and Company, including Molly Bloom, Mary Beth Constant, Alex Foster, and Emily Mahar, whose labor and expertise helped shape this novel.

My agent, Jessica Kasmer-Jacobs, and her colleagues at the Deborah Harris Agency who supported and protected me and my work in ways they're probably too humble to acknowledge.

Claire Messud, who, since I first staggered into her workshop as a college sophomore, has been a compassionate guide and a constant source of inspiration and encouragement.

The Departments of English and Art, Film, and Visual Studies at Harvard University. I'd like to thank Teju Cole, Alfred Guzzetti, Robb Moss, Neel Mukherjee, and Dominga Sotomayor for their thoughtful feedback; Ezra Block, Michael Bronski, Lauren Bimmler, Jimmy Hung, Peter Sacks, and Paula Soares for their kindness; and Jack Megan and the Office for the Arts for their support.

Every teacher who believed in me and told me I should read and write. I'd like to thank three women—legends— in particular: Yuyu Eytan, who taught me that, contrary to popular belief, history is an art; Orit Schwarz-Franco, who pushed me to pose the questions that terrify me most; and Ruthi Ben-Dor, who introduced me to Arnold van Gennep's *Rites of Passage*, an anthropological masterpiece that granted this book its tripartite structure.

The Rhodes Trust and St John's College at the University of Oxford. I'm particularly grateful to Mary Eaton, Elizabeth Kiss, Doron Weber, and the folks at Rhodes House, who provided me with the best circumstances for deep thinking any writer could hope for.

The staff at the London Library, my peers at the Emerging Writers Programme, and the extraordinary Claire Berliner, one of my favorite London Jews.

My many housemates during the writing of this book, including Emma Choi, Lauren Fadiman, Saul Glist, Natasha

Lasky, Isabel Levin, Sophie Li, Rosa Rahimi Aminzavvar, Elliot Schiff, Freddie Shanel, Sasha Tinelli, Liv Weinstein, and Eden Amare Yitbarek. Owen Torrey offered me his sage advice and emotional support. The Dudley Co-Op, a.k.a. the Center for High-Energy Metaphysics, and its fabulous residents throughout my years there gave me a precious space to breathe and learn, for which I remain grateful.

The phenomenal members of the crew and cast who collaborated with me on the short film version of *Mazeltov* and the many kind souls whose generosity had made it possible.

My beloved friends around the world, whose care, wisdom, and talent are imprinted on every page of this novel. I'm deeply indebted to Che Applewhaite, Frank Cahill, Chloe Claudel, Joshua Cohen, Dafi Cramer, Shahar Kramer, Thomas Peermohamed Lambert, Kelly Lloyd, Freddie Mac-Bruce, Uri Meir, Nanak Narulla, Jordan Osserman, Jack Parlett, Tamar Peled, Molly Peterson, Von Pitts, Mitch Polonsky, May Resh, Lily Scherlis, Nir Segal, Marc Sutton, Yehonatan Vilozny, Kenza Wilks, Freya Willis, Lee Yaron, and Itai Zwecker for their keen observations and wise counsel. This book was written in loving memory of Laura Lambez and Tarin Shalfy, who are in my heart forever. Special thanks to Layan Deeb, Amir Khoury, and Lamma Mansour for their openheartedness and insight; Tom Sidi, who has been reminding me not to take myself too seriously since kindergarten; and Gaya Segal, my chosen sister, who makes everything, including *Mazeltov*, feasible and worthwhile.

My family—*Ima*, *Aba*, Yuvi, Adamiko, Nonna, Uri, and

Daphna, as well as our dear relatives on Paros and in Batzra, Paris, Salerno, Toronto, and elsewhere—who fill my life with joy, love, and compassion, even from a distance. They are everywhere in these pages and in my world. *Ani ohev ethchem.*

Four years ago, I began to write a letter to the boy I was at thirteen, timid and perplexed and curious. That letter morphed into this book. I'd like to offer it to that kid—and all the kids who, like him, mistakenly believe they're broken—alongside a line from Leonard Cohen, an old-time favorite: "There is a crack, a crack in everything / That's how the light gets in."

About the Author

Eli Zuzovsky holds degrees from Harvard and Oxford, where he studied as a Rhodes Scholar. In 2022, he was selected for the *Forbes* Israel 30 Under 30 list and the London Library Emerging Writers Programme, and he is the winner of the 2025 Einstein Fellowship. His films and plays have been shown at the New York Jewish Film Festival, Boston's Museum of Fine Arts, the American Repertory Theater, and the Edinburgh Festival Fringe, among others. He currently lives in London. *Mazeltov* is his first novel.